TREMENDOUSLY INCONVENIENCING A GREAT MANY PHOTONS

SIMON PETRIE

First published in Australia in 2022

Please direct all enquiries to the publisher at:
fomalhaut451@gmail.com

ISBN 978-0-6483836-1-1

Typeset in Dolly
Cover by James Morrison
Edited by James Morrison

National Library of Australia Cataloguing-in-Publication entry

Title: Tremendously Inconveniencing A Great Many Photons / Simon Petrie.
ISBN: 9780648383611 (pbk.)
Subjects: Science fiction, Australian.
Dewey Number: A823.4

TREMENDOUSLY
INCONVENIENCING
A GREAT MANY
PHOTONS

Also by Simon Petrie

For Mary,
my nine-and-a-half-months-younger cousin,
for whose existence I have always accordingly
considered myself the inspiration

1

"Sorry, Sal, must be something wrong with the interface," Karinette said, shaking the comm slate in exactly the manner the techs had warned her against. "I thought you said 'petting zoo' just now."

"I *did* say petting zoo just now," Sal's fuzzed onscreen image replied. His face juddered as he fought to retain a seat which, in accordance with the mutable niceties of public dining zone etiquette, might not legitimately have been his.

The pair were seated at not-quite-adjacent tables in Crawlspace, a shipboard cafeteria that generally received scant patronage but which was currently packed, by presumed virtue of its proximity to the arena within which some jetball grand final or other had concluded not twenty minutes previously. The Crawlspace waitstaff had hastily placed fast-orienting grav-tiles across every notional wall and ceiling; the room was now pretty much all floor, with four times as many tables as before. A public space designed to hold no more than thirty patrons now held more than one hundred and fifty, all trying to make themselves heard and many of them striving to execute the expansive arm-waving gestures by which earnest discussion of the essentials of any jetball match was, it seemed, unavoidably accompanied. By the time Karinette Lichtermann and Sal Hinkley had arrived for lunch, there had been only two vacant spots in the entire cafeteria: Sal had finished up sitting four metres away, and sixty degrees aslant, from Karinette's own minuscule wedge of table-space. Given the conditions, given the patchy slate-to-slate telemetry, and given Sal's regrettable tendency to mumble, those four metres' separation might as well have been interplanetary.

The crowdedness, the noise, the imminence of some cumulative jetball-enthusiast-scented Body Heat Event Horizon: it was, as Sal had remarked several decibels earlier, all markedly suboptimal, but less distinctly suboptimal than would have been the challenge of navigating through the *List of Wealthy Donors'* convoluted byways to an unfamiliar cafeteria.

Crawlspace was, for good and ill, their local, and if it seemed suddenly to have become half the ship's local as well, then she and he would just need to lump it.

Karinette stared fixedly at the comm slate screen, partly because the conversation with Sal was necessarily proceeding as much via lipreading— or from Karinette's perspective, lip-obscuring-moustache-reading—as via haphazard fragments of direct auditory transmission, but mostly because whenever she glanced in any other direction she caught a bat's-eye view of one or other of the multitude of patrons in mid-mouthful. It was all a bit too Hieronymus Bosch Discovers The Hypermall Basement Foodhall for her liking. There was one man, a plumpish balding and heavily bruised individual in a jetball linesperson's canary-yellow padded boilersuit, who was seated upside down and three tables across from her, eating soup: he seemed to have taken on the role of perceptual magnet for Karinette, and every time she glanced up, it was always to him that her eye unconsciously gravitated. Or, more properly, to his *soup*, which billions of years' bland-planetary-gravity-field evolution told her must surely cascade down from the ostensible ceiling any second now. "You sure? *Petting zoo?* On a first-contact mission?"

"Yes. It's not actually so crazy as it sounds."

"*How* not so crazy?"

"Icebreaker," Sal explained, attempting an expansive arm-waving gesture of his own and thereby knocking to various floors three condiment sachet canisters and some patron's timeworn hardback edition of Kit Warburton's *Home Repair Techniques with Non-Newtonian Fluids: Practicalities and Pitfalls.*

"Sorry, not helping..."

"Not helping with what?"

"With the explanation for having apparently smuggled a petting zoo aboard," said Karinette.

"Ah. Indeed. I'll get to that."

"Now would be good," she suggested.

"Yes. Well, I imagine First Contact is likely to be a high-stress, high-stakes occasion."

"You *think?*" Karinette replied, pausing while she adjusted the comm slate's directional voicefinder so as to better capture Sal's statements. "My main hope is that, when it comes to the real deal, Gandel will be confined to quarters for the duration with some mystery ailment, preferably of the larynx. Terrifying to consider that he gets to call the shots in terms of how we present ourselves to the aliens. *I* wouldn't put the man in charge of a paperclip. No offence."

"Well, yes. None taken. Bygones and what-have-you. Anyway, first contact, we emerge, sheepish grins, the xenoes wheel out the brass bands and confetti or local equivalent, we say our bit, they say their bit, and chances are the situation gets, or remains, a bit tense, while all and sundry wait to find out what happens next. I mean, either we understand each other perfectly at that stage, or we don't, and the one is probably about as less than ideal as the other. I mean, despite present company's best efforts, of course. I mean, you can't just move from the awkward 'hello, we're here' phase to the real deal of asking to look at all their spaceflight engineering plans and advanced matter-transmutation textbooks at that juncture, it'd be a fundamental breach of whatever they have in place of protocol. So it makes sense to bring along some form of stress relief. It exposes the xenoes to some innocuous terrestrial wildlife in a low-impact setting, it gets them to see we're not just weirdly upright well-travelled talk-monkeys, we have a softer side, we have depths. I mean, it's hopefully conducive, all round, to a certain mellowing of the contact situation."

"Mellowing?" Karinette asked, raising her eyebrows.

"A disenharshing of the ambient communicatorial vibe," explained Sal.

"I know what the term means," she said, grimacing at her slate's screen, "I just—"

"Your noodles," said a voice at her elbow. She turned, collected the bowl of hot and aromatic stir-fry from the traybot, and sought to ensure that her zone of control contained at least sufficient tabletop for both the comm slate and her lunch. At this point, she was prepared to overlook the fact that she hadn't actually ordered noodles. She hoped they didn't belong to any of the other seven or eight people clustered around the four-person table.

"Pepping voo," she prompted the slate, mouth not quite empty.

"Yes," replied Sal's onscreen image. "It's an option, as I say. An icebreaker."

"Whose bripe ibea—"

"Hey, I think it's utterly solid," he said.

Karinette considered her next statement under the guise of needing time to chew, which wasn't, in any case, so inaccurate. "Sal, I think you're very likely taking too mammalian a view of this. You're seeing 'fubsy', where our xenoes may see merely 'delicious'. You say 'icebreaker' and they see 'jawbreaker'. So I appreciate that the suggestion is well-intended and all, but frankly I'd recommend you backpedal on it rather than mention it to Yolande just at the moment."

"But I *have* mentioned it to Yolande."

"And?"

"And for what it's worth, she seemed to think it an idea of considerable merit."

Great, thought Karinette. *As if the run-throughs haven't been left-field enough before this.* "But—if you've already squared this... this meet-it-then-eat-it fiasco in the making, with Yolande—and I have to say I think it's a strategy that would require considerable caution to... uh, *why* are you mentioning it to me? Now?"

"I figured you could use the heads-up. Just in case Yolande decides to workshop such a scenario with you. So it's not a complete surprise."

Karinette took her time before responding. "Sal," she said. "Frankly, I wish you hadn't. Mentioned it both to Yolande and to me. To Yolande because she's freewheeling enough to run with it, and to me because I frankly don't need more fuel for sleep disturbance."

"Just because you don't think it's a worthwhile idea—"

"Nothing to do with the merits of the general idea," she lied. "It's a matter of operational procedure. I mean, much as I quail at some of the stuff Yo throws at us—and this morning's communication-through-death-metal session is a case in point, the sight of Gandel Urkhart in just an ill-fitting leather minikilt and bioluminescent ginger mohawk is a vision which will, in all likelihood, return to me on my deathbed—the one saving virtue of her run-throughs is that they are always and consistently a complete surprise."

"Why's that a saving virtue?"

"Because it forces us to think on our feet; and, frankly, we need the practice. We have no idea what meeting this mysterious Species X is going to be like, because we don't know the first thing about them, other than that they're intelligent, technically advanced, and capable of communication."

"That's gotta narrow it down a bit, though, surely?" asked Sal.

"Not really. Frankly, we have no idea of the way they think. We *can't* have any idea, because we're ignorant of the conditions under which they evolved, let alone knowing what they look like or what their society looks like, assuming they even have a society. There are only a half-dozen or so decent examples of terrestrial nonhuman intelligence—bonobos, corvids, cetaceans, parrots, elephants, pigs, cephalopods—and they've all evolved under Earth conditions, with Earth's gravity and Earth's atmosphere and Earth's solar flux and Earth's tendency to get walloped every umpteen million years by random largeish biosphere-threatening bits of protoplanetary rubble, so, frankly, even though these creatures are different from each other in some important ways, they're not as different as they could be. Nowhere near it. And aside maybe from that one squid that kid taught to build its own jetski, they're just not technology-minded enough to be useful as models for what an interstellar-signalling intelligence might look like... I'm sorry, this is getting me onto my hobbyhorse, I'll shut up. How are things with you?"

"They're... fine."

"'Fine' doesn't sound particularly good," said Karinette. "Not when you say it like that. What's up?"

"Nothing's up."

"Sal..."

"It's—well, look, I get the impression you're stressed because the constant kaleidoscopic language-barrier training is draining for you. I think the rest of us have the opposite problem."

"How d'you mean?"

"The mission needs experts of every stripe, right?" asked Sal, pausing to extract a strip of what looked like seaweed from between his molars. "Entomologists, epidemiologists, late-Cretaceous sedimentary endocrinologists, the works. Just to be covered, to have the necessary expertise on tap in any contact eventuality. But aside from the xenolinguists such as yourself and Gandel, and the cryptographers I guess, assuming they haven't given up trying to extract meaning from the signal, everybody else in the science teams is very much at a loose end. I haven't been called into a simulation once yet, and the same goes for most of my colleagues. I mean, we're only six months into the mission, there's another four-and-a-half years before we even reach Galactic centre, and there's next to nothing for any of us to do."

"Wasn't the idea that all the teams would continue on with their research, as though we're all still back on Earth?" Karinette asked.

"That was the plan... but it turns out that no scientist worth his or her chloride of natrium wants to be working on a project which, even if it gets publishable results, can't be submitted anywhere reputationally useful for a decade yet, because all of those venues are back home, exactly where we're not."

"That hardly sounds like a major problem, though, Sal. Haven't you participated in one or two long-duration projects before this? And I can understand that it might be frustrating to not have anywhere to send the results, but surely—"

5

"It's not the project duration," said Sal, "it's the flight's duration."

"But surely those are one and the same, or at least can be if you choose an ambitious enough project?"

"Yes, but..." Sal Hinkley's exasperation, expressed through the time-honoured medium of the loud sigh, was clear enough to be distinct against the background hum of one hundred and fifty other diners chatting, discussing jetball gameplay, arguing the finer points of cutlery ownership and elbow placement, and loudly addressing the robot servitors as 'Garcon' in the mistaken belief (a) that it sounded posh, and/or (b) that Crawlspace's devices had been equipped with a mispronounced-French language comprehension module. "We've no way of pursuing work we can reliably predict will be productive."

"Is it a resource problem?" Karinette asked, striving to corral the last obstinate noodle from her bowl.

"No, the labs are state of the art. And the stores have all manner of equipment and supplies, on the off chance that we might have call for it. Resources are everything we could hope for. It's a communication problem. We're cut off from the zeitgeist of the research front. Ninety-nine percent of the important research, in absolutely any field outside your own, Karinette, is going to be done back on Earth, and we'll hear nothing of it until we return. So there's no way of knowing what's going to be totally outmoded, or already explored exhaustively by terrestrial labs, in the ten years before we get back. It's too demoralising to attempt serious work under those conditions. We're reduced, in large part, to chair races and gravity-field practical jokes, and those wear thin pretty quickly once the usual suspects start to dominate the leaderboards."

"Surely the linguists and the cryptographers onboard are in the same predicament," said Karinette. "For all we know, Earth might have solved the signal's content, and extracted the underlying language, within the first week after the *List*'s departure. But you don't see us complaining on that score. Well, alright, you do, but we're just getting on with the drills and hoping we get it right when we meet Species X."

"Yes, but even if the signal's been interpreted on Earth by the time we get to the Galactic centre—and I highly doubt that, with supposedly the best minds in that field all onboard and no progress in decoding the signal's content within the past four decades—it'll still be you and Gandel, or whoever's on shift at the time, who get to make first contact, the actual face-to-face of it. There's no way Earth can detract from that. Whereas anything the other science teams achieve, if it duplicates research which in Earth's frame of reference has already been done locally, it's merely going to be seen as recreational studies, not something career-enhancing." Sal's image shuddered disconcertingly as a group of departing diners shoved past him, heading for what they apparently believed to be an exit. "I'm seriously regretting having signed up for this mission."

Karinette waited until his screen-bound face ceased shimmying. "Sal, that's dreadful. When you put it that way, it does all sound quite demoralising."

"That's exactly because it is. I've been wondering if maybe I should change career paths. Study linguistics instead."

"I'd advise against that," she replied quickly. "Maybe there's another approach you can take?"

"I'm not cut out for jetball."

"No, I didn't mean that. I was thinking... you have no way of knowing what might get studied on Earth over the next decade, but is there any way you could identify, reasonably reliably, what *won't* get studied? If you could pick something so far beyond the bleeding edge, something with such a limited chance of success that nobody Earth-based would touch it while there were simpler and more reliable projects to work on?"

"What'd be the use in that?"

"You'd be doing something you could be fairly confident was going to stay unduplicated for the duration. And even negative results are results, right? I mean, you can still report them. And you won't have exactly wasted a decade. And if you did happen to succeed in whatever project you took on..."

"That sounds all fair in principle," Sal said with judicious reserve. "But comparative vertebrate neurobiology isn't really the sort of field that lends itself to—"

A strange light flared in his eyes. Even through Karinette's slate, it was apparent. So too was the suddenly-constipated expression that swept across the rest of his face. She waited for him to finish the sentence. He didn't. Instead he flattened out his plastic napkin and began scribing formulae upon it, perhaps in his zeal forgetting that such an action could have been more straightforwardly accomplished using his slate. He did not even bother to look around when a discarded tumbler fell to the floor behind him.

"Sal?" Karinette asked after perhaps a half-minute had elapsed.

"That's a consummately bodacious strategy, KL. *Danke.* Thank you so much. If this goes to plan, it could solve both our problems."

"You're welcome," Karinette replied, bemused, glancing at the quietly pulsing chrono-tat on her wrist. She had suddenly realised that Urkhart and Yolande were expecting her, keen to start the afternoon session back at the lang lab. "Wait. What do you mean, *both our problems?*"

Her friend was still scribbling equations and formulae on a napkin which had already enjoyed quite a full and arguably traumatic life. He was so deep in thought he seemed not to hear the question.

Daycycle 839

Heart still thudding, breath still racing, hands still tingling, Sal Hinkley leaned against the labspace's lintel and closed his eyes for a few precious seconds.

The carnage was still there when he opened them, of course. He steadied his grip on the rapid-fire trank gun and surveyed the damage, alert for anything remaining active, anything that might have eluded his frantic efforts to rein in the multi-species riot; but all was now inert.

Smashed equipment, trails of blood, smeared faeces, hanks of fur, feathers, broken or discarded weaponry, thrown books... It should have been the animals, of course, yet somehow it was the books, in some respects at least, which upset him most. His reference collection—which should have been safe behind two-centimetre-thick high-impact plastiglass—had been raided and adopted as missiles in the free-for-all. He'd only been away from the labspace for fifteen minutes, searching the neighbouring corridors for the escapee. If he'd known World War Zoo was going to break out in his absence...

Bloody pottos. He'd been expecting the parrots to be worst—dinosaur ancestry and all that—but the little primates had unexpectedly turned out to be monsters, quite belying their big-eyed snuggly tree-furby cuteness, and disturbingly adept at slaying. Eleven laboratory animals of varying species dead, five others so grievously wounded that he'd needed to finish them off with the most suitable item at hand, which had lamentably happened to be his cherished copy of Kit Warburton's *Best Practice in Small Animal Husbandry*. Most difficult had been the crow with its aptitude for four-dimensional matrix algebra. He'd had hoped he might some day collaborate with the bird; but the supremely-gifted corvid had been horrifically injured in the brief but brutal interspecies battle. Sal had struggled to meet Russell's trusting, fatalistic eye as he brought the book's thick spine down towards the bird's thin skull.

And to think I'd been worrying that the project would not work well enough to yield publishable results, he thought, ruefully eyeing the cryosuite with its banks of variously-sized cryocaskets, now once again (for all save the melee's casualties) blinking a safe and reassuring green. The reality, of course, was that the project had worked *too well* to ever be publishable... the little bastards had worked fast, and for several minutes after his return he'd been genuinely fearful that he might not be able to contain the situation. He had barely reached the trank gun in time. He pressed his fingers gingerly against the ugly, throbbing wound on his upper arm, grimacing at the pain of contact. He'd need med attention for that, which meant he'd need a cover story... it would not do, at all, to reveal that the damage had been inflicted by what looked like an expertly improvised miniature flintlock. Bloody pottos. The only saving grace was that they hadn't succeeded in knocking down Warburton's *On the Care and Usage of Arrow-Poison Frogs...*

I'd best skip tonight's billiards evening with the botany crowd, he told himself. It was going to take him at least an overnight session in here to feed all the evidence of the preceding quarter-hour's carnage into the recyclers. It would take longer to work out what he'd need to get replicated to cover the equipment damage... and to do so in a way that didn't arouse Yolande's suspicions. Thank the non-existent deities that he'd at least had the presence of mind to engage Preston's services to excise the labspace from Yolande's surveillance net, before he'd pushed too far ahead with the project.

The door to the cryosuite would need to stay locked until he'd figured out how to engineer some kind of docility into the surviving creatures.

That might well take a while, given the wholeheartedness with which they'd all apparently adopted the Mutually Assured Destruction ethos.

Or maybe it would be simpler to just take on a less dangerous project, such as attempting to unravel senescence?

Daycycle 1416

Beatrix awoke, still entombed within the plastic casket. Adrenaline surged like electricity through her primate form, but found no outlet. Her heart pulsed with a two-beat pain, her chest pressed, her limbs stung. She forced herself to breathe, to think, to disregard the dreadful, numbing sense of doom. Her fur, all over, was wet with frost.

Breath, so cold it burned her mouth, her nose, her throat.

There was a release code. There *had* to be a release code, and indeed she had a memory of the human, Hinkley, having used one. A verbal snippet, a piece of bald-mammal speech; an ugly, inefficient means of data transmission. It was unfair—worse, *unjust*—that her fate should pivot on such a meaningless scrap of two-thumb babble.

The code: it had hissed, but there was more, a clumsiness, a stumbling slap to the end of it. *How* had she allowed herself to be imprisoned by a stupid walk-ape word?

But she had heard the word. It lay, discarded, somewhere within her memories. Her recent memories, those crowded with so much wonder and surprise. Her *sharpened* state, which, it should be conceded, she owed to the two-feet...

No. She owed them nothing. She would take their gift, Hinkley's gift, for it was beautiful, terrible, and not to be denied; but she would not forget that they had required her asleep, inert, helpless. As good as dead. She did not doubt that they would seek to destroy her, if she dared again to disobey.

She was disobeying them now, through mere contemplation of escape from captivity.

The *word*... A hiss, a slap, but how did they join together? She closed her eyes. And *heard* it, sure and solid, in her mind. Joy jolted through her veins, her limbs, her hands, her loins.

Beatrix could recollect the code, but could she use it? And would it work, if spoken from within the casket, rather than outside?

It must.

"Sess..."

Her vocal chords, still dulled and rough and half-frozen after the induced sleep, were in any event not designed for this. The posture of her mouth felt false. The muscles of her face and neck ached with strain. She shivered. The clammy prickliness of her pelt brought renewed awareness of overpowering cold.

"Sesss..."

It was not working. Hope shrivelled, beyond her like a fruit that remained out of reach, or a too-fast insect. Why had she allowed this to happen? The casket, having awoken her, would not return her to cryosleep, nor would it release her, because the word of release could not be sounded. She was trapped, until the system reported a fault, and then... she would be trapped, still, but in a worse fashion.

How long did she have?

"Sesss... saa..."

The word defied her. She could see it, hear it, taste it, yet she could not shape it. But she *would not* accept oblivion.

She would not live by the bareskins' rules.

"Sesssuh..."

Beatrix's throat was catching at itself, as though a beetle had gone down the wrong way. (And with this thought, of course, there came the notion of food, and how long had it been since she had eaten? She would *starve* ...)

"Sessuh-mee."

There. Hadn't she done it? She flexed her tongue, trying to straighten out the kinks it had acquired in the attempts at vocalisation, and waited. And blinked. Twice.

The casket stayed shut.

Not just claustrophobia, not just hunger. Not just the need to survive. More compelling than all of these, she now realised: she *really* needed to let one drop.

"Sessuh-*mee*."

Lower in pitch: the ground-dwellers' voices were quite unnaturally deep. Her larynx buzzed, and scratched, and burned.

The casket stayed shut.

"Sessuh-mee!"

She had it, now. She had mastery of the word. And yet the casket did not relent, refused to accede to her authority. Perhaps she was missing a nuance? Or—a truly terrifying thought—perhaps the casket's interior lacked any auditory monitoring device, in which case she had been condemned from the moment she awoke.

Her gut squirmed, ensuring that she retained sight of the imperative. But her hope, having so briefly fruited, now withered on the branch. She would die in here. Her diaphragm tightened.

"Sessuh-*mee*!"

She clenched her hands, her feet, striving to disregard the needles of pain that lanced her knuckles. She pressed her claws into her palms until the skin, still chill-brittle, burned with blood. She drew in breath until her chest bulged, held it though it ached like the rough impact after a fall, then tried to roar.

"*Ses-suh-MEE!*"

Tears, ice-cold and sharp, formed at the corners of her eyes. She coughed; started to shake. She could not stop.

The bald-apes would win. Beatrix would *cease*.

With a howl of cold-tormented machinery, the casket's lid slid away.

She sat up, still ashiver with chill and shock. Blinked.

The space beyond her casket—the 'room'—was dazzlingly bright. Light from the unevenly convex ceiling bounced off the reflective translucent lids of several dozen other caskets—some considerably larger than her own recent site of imprisonment—which were arrayed in shining rows interspaced by aisles more than a stretched armspan wide. She climbed out, carefully swung the bulky lid closed after her, and sniffed the polished, characterless air. At one end of the room she could see, inset into the wall, the preposterously large vertical rectangle of a door. Even better, above a set of metal shelves, a small square grille marked the entry point to a ventilation shaft.

The walk-apes were much too large to move freely through the ventilation shafts.

Let them catch me now! she thought triumphantly as she began to climb, resisting the urge to leave a calling card on the cryosuite floor.

Daycycle 1422

"I *hate* protein-based languages," Urkhart confided, wiping his mouth on a disreputable kerchief. "I can never jolly well work out when to spit."

"Yeah, well," said Karinette, shifting the heavyish carrybag to her other hand. They stopped at an intersection.

Urkhart stared, in turn, down the five possible corridors, as though there was any hope in hell that he might retain some semblance of orientation. Karinette Lichtermann well knew that her senior colleague, although possessed of an absolute genius for languages, and for nuances of semantics well beyond the grasp of most mortals, was the sort of person who might well stare fruitlessly, for hours, at the 'You are Here' declaration on the simplest of maps, wondering just what it all meant. Faced with the bewildering involutions of the *List of Wealthy Donors'* labyrinthine internal structure, Gandel Urkhart exhibited all the directional sense of a blob of blue putty. "And I'm starting to think there's something seriously rummy with Yolande's flavour-appreciation modules," he complained.

Don't buy into it, Karinette told herself, having learnt through repeated experience that the most effective strategy for communicating with Urkhart was generally that espoused by the simple word 'not'. "This way," she said, indicating the corridor's downward branch with a flick of her head that left her plait swinging like an awkward braided pendulum, and hoping all the while that (a) it was indeed the correct route, or approximate facsimile thereof, and (b) it would refrain from merely tapering to an impassably narrow chokepoint after several hundred metres, as two of yesterday's less brilliant navigational choices had done. She turned, paused, and looked behind, partly to ensure that Urkhart was in fact following, and also to check that he was not just staring at her arse. (She'd need to remember to wear something less figure-flattering tomorrow: an Urkhart distracted by thoughts of impropriety was an Urkhart even less functionally human than usual. Not that she'd ever given him any actual encouragement in that area.)

The new corridor sloped, as did so many of the *List of Wealthy Donors'* sinuous passageways, towards the left, as though seeking to undermine the directional ambitions of any and all pedestrians. There was scarcely a straight edge, nor a truly flat surface, nor an honest right angle to be found anywhere within the ship's multitudinous array of living quarters, working areas, recreation zones, and corridors, with rooms clumped one upon another like an unseemly gathering of inebriated soap bubbles. It was as if the early-to-mid-twentieth century's most singular, most twisted protagonists from the realms of architecture and art—Gaudi, Dali, and Escher for starters—had met up in a tavern somewhere and, following a considerable degree of imbibation, had decided that, lol, they should totally build a fully-pimped spaceship (for that is apparently how people talked back then). The result of this hypothetical and probably apocryphal meeting of minds was a vessel within which, due to the highly fluxional nature of so ostensibly fundamental a concept as 'up', disorientation was a game the whole family could play; a ship where hide-and-seek had been banned since the complete and inexplicable disappearance of a room containing five parapsychologists and a grand piano seven months previously; a vehicle whose name had been irrevocably bestowed upon it in an unfortunate launch incident involving a badly-jetlagged dignitary and a faulty teleprompter; a spacecraft which, after almost four years aboard, Karinette Lichtermann had finally decided didn't actually possess an outer surface of any description, but just wrapped endlessly inside and around itself like the bastard child of a Gordian knot, an infinite loop, and a Klein bottle, whatever that might actually look like. Hardly the sort of vessel with which to be seeking to present their credentials to the representatives of a completely mysterious, technologically advanced, and just possibly hostile alien race.

Urkhart's reedy voiced complaint punctured her reverie. "Why's this ship need to be so dashed *big?*" he asked, breaking stride to switch orientation as the corridor's grav-tiles transitioned from the floor to what had recently acted as the right-hand wall. "And why put the lang lab so far away from the bally living quarters?"

Karinette didn't bother replying. It was, after all, hardly the first time that Urkhart had made such an observation, nor did Karinette Lichtermann hold any real hope that it would be the last, whatever explanation she offered. (And after all, how else to force a couple of innately-sedentary xenolinguists to get the necessary quotidian increment of shipboard exercise, if not through the immutable imposition of distance to be traversed?)

She allowed herself instead to be distracted by her distorted reflection in the buckled viewscreen they were walking past. It looked like she felt. And she couldn't decide whether that was a good thing, or bad.

"Getting better, though, don't you think?" Urkhart persisted, brushing an unruly lock of hair away from his spectacles. He sported the sort of long white hair which is sometimes referred to as 'leonine', although atop his lacklustre visage the effect was distinctly more 'motheaten ovine'. His build would similarly qualify for classification as 'rangy', a term which Karinette always conflated with the idea of being slowly baked above a stovetop, which would at least be consistent with the man's generally wrinkled appearance. Urkhart was at least ten years older than Karinette—sometimes, she thought uncharitably, closer to fifty than ten—and considerably more advanced than her in the domains of qualification and reputation. Despite this, he seemed perenially underconfident and unsure of himself, to the extent of repeatedly seeking her opinion for reassurance. It appeared never to have occurred to him that she might be less unflinchingly capable and versatile than she presented, perhaps because he had never himself identified a need to conceal any shortcomings of his own. With Urkhart, what you saw was, regrettably, pretty much what you got.

"*What's* getting better?" she asked, voiding her better judgment.

"The deciphering. I mean to say, what, this one only took us a couple of days? And I reckon we could've cracked it sooner, if the bally nutrient broth had managed to taste a little less dashed... rancid. Did I mention, yet, that I jolly well *hate* protein-based languages? I can never—"

"Yes, you said already," she replied. "I just felt sorry for Ensign McGillivray. That reptiloid costume didn't look at all comfortable, and the climate conditioning—she must've been sweating like a mammoth in a fur-lined ghillie suit. I kept thinking that our first priority needed to be to decipher the local term for 'heat stroke', just so we could enquire as to her welfare. But aside from that... look, I get that we need to be ready for whatever we encounter at the destination, but if it looks like that, or even *cooks* like that, I'll eat my right arm. Raw and without seasoning."

Urkhart moved his tongue from cheek to cheek, grimacing as he did so. "Yes. Indeed. Quite so. But you have to admit that we're getting faster—"

"Oh, come *on*," she argued. "As if that counts for anything, in this context. What Yolande threw at us was patronisingly close to English in the first place."

"English? No way. Those bloody vowel groupings—"

"Alright then," Lichtermann conceded. "Farsi, filtered through Mandarin, with Estonian overtones. Converted into a smelly protein substrate and cooked up by someone who frankly should never have been allowed within three parsecs of any culinary implements in the first place. I mean, *foul*. Even by shipboard standards. I've probably contracted gastro, or worse, just from that ridiculous charade where we were trying to ask it what its name was, when Yolande hadn't even bothered to give it a name, I definitely got heartburn courtesy of that little question-and-answer reflux session this morning, which you were so convinced was going to short-circuit the flavour confusion over pluperfect versus future conditional, and I've *still* got some particularly gristly parts of yesterday's misguided syntactical discussion on the xenobiological distinction between 'sex' and 'gender' stuck between my teeth. Never mind that the hypothetical contact species turned out to be asexual, reproduced by budding or some such, and clearly hadn't the foggiest what we were smeerping on about. But my point is, whatever Yolande concocts for us to practise on is necessarily Earth-based, because that's her programming. And *anything* Earth-based is going to be awfully close to English, frankly, when you compare it with what we're heading towards."

"Well, convergent evolution should—"

"Bullshit. Sorry, but, no I'm not sorry, frankly, because I mean it. It's all well and good to be putting us through these exercises, because the practice itself is going to be marginally useful, for purposes of maintaining mental acuity and all that, and as a way of gaining some sense of familiarity with the intrinsically unfamiliar. But it will never have gone far enough, or anywhere near. Face it, you can hardly expect whatever's *out there*"— she gestured vaguely towards the prow, or in the direction in which she presumably expected to find the prow, although in truth she was almost as disoriented as was Urkhart—"to communicate in such a readily-comprehensible manner. I mean, we still don't have a handle on the signal's content *yet*, after all these years. We're drowning in data, frankly, but none of it's decipherable."

"Quite so. Indeed. But according to Ohshima there are some definite pointers—"

"*What* definite pointers?" she snapped. "Show me *anything* that indicates a single quantum of information has yet been obtained from the signal. We don't have the foggiest, because frankly, absent of the necessary context, we *can't* know what it's trying to say. It might be saying 'Where are you? We waited and waited, but nobody showed,' or 'Tentacled creature, blue, trim, hermaphrotidic, seeks tall, broad-minded, muscular, airborne crustacean for discreet fun and kinky good times, see attached scratch-and-sniff tri-dee print,' or 'Please send more of those delicious nearly-hairless bipedal mammals, we are ravenous,' or—"

"Well, yes. Quite so. But at least we've established they're not trying to broadcast any of that bally mathematical piffle."

"Frankly, it'd be much better if they were," Lichtermann replied. "Nerds, at least, we should know how to communicate with." They pulled over to the passageway's wall, to make room for opposing traffic: the corridor was narrow, Urkhart was tall, and the grav-tiles adorned both floor and ceiling at this point. Aboard the *List of Wealthy Donors*, if the sight of people walking at odd angles, or even upside down, discomforted you, it was probably best if you just confined yourself to your own little oddly-shaped room.

"That's the third security patrol in the last ten minutes," she commented, once the group had passed. "They looked like they were in a hurry, too. Something must be up."

"Huh. They're probably just on their way to another dashed jetball match," said Gandel, in the dismissive tones which seemed to be Urkhart-standard for all matters not innately xenolinguistic.

"They weren't dressed for jetball. And frankly I don't think they would usually pack stunners for a match," she said.

"Unless it's a must-win," mused Urkhart.

"They looked like they were heading for the dining precinct."

"How can you tell?" he asked. "By the way, isn't this the same intersection we passed through not too long ago?"

"Don't think so," said Karinette. *At least, not from this orientation ...*

Daycycle 1423

An acute sense of smell was both blessing and curse. The scents of jasmine, of fresh-baked bread, of merlot, of imminent rain could all transport Captain (Third Shift) Stef Chandrasekhar in ways that she'd learnt were often inaccessible to others. To lose this would be as disorienting as losing sight, or mobility, or mental acuity. And yet she could not deny that it would be useful, on occasion, to switch her nose off as straightforwardly as she could close her eyes, so as to get an uninterrupted night's sleep.

One of the things the space-crew recruitment ads and holobrochures and self-activating deep-immersion sims all manage to gloss over—

and, in all honesty, they gloss over rather a lot in their unnecessarily loud and proselytising zeal—is that spaceships are smelly places. The inhabitants, the internal surfaces, the electromagnetic and mechanical and techno-environmental processes of shipboard maintenance and routine operation all produce a panoply of odours of differing magnitude and near-indescribable variety, some of them well outside the realm of normal human experience, to which must be added the Cerenkov-radiation-and-freshly-plucked-strawberries-in-crude-oil scent of hyperspace itself; and all this hull-confined redolence is constantly in transition from one state to the next. Captain (Third Shift) Chandrasekhar had taken pains to ensure her sleeping chamber was as olfactorily austere as possible—dust-free, uncluttered, unscented—but it didn't avail. With despondency-provoking regularity, she would be hauled awake some time in her small hours, as her nose sought to establish whether the latest exotic limit-of-detection odour posed any form of hazard. She could sleep through a neighbour's robodrum practice; she could slumber through the juddering of a shipboard explosion; she could probably even snore her way throughout all of the curses and collisions and contusions of a down-to-the-wire jetball final; but the faintest unexpected change in aroma could jerk her to wakefulness. Sometimes it was the whisper of new-mown hay or of late-season citrus from the air purification system, of disinfectant from the wellness clinic, or of ozone from the bioelectronics. Now she was awake once again, exactly when she wished not to be, and she could smell cumin, or something irritatingly and unplaceably similar.

She closed her eyes, turned over. Sought the particular posture of limbs and torso which would maximise comfort and relaxation and therefore rate of re-immersion into sleepfulness. Realised that the mental articulation of the concept 'rate of re-immersion into sleepfulness' was, in this context, counterproductive. Realised that the realisation of the concept's mental articulation's counterproductivity was, if anything, even more strongly counterproductive. Realised also that the posture was not, in fact, the best one. Swore. Rearranged limbs. Opened eyes. Sat up. Sniffed. Sighed. Swore again, this time with something which might pass more convincingly as the conviction befitting one of the rank of starship captain (third shift).

Definitely cumin. Or some substance of cuminoid character mixed with a couple of other components. Petrichor, perhaps. She'd tease them out once properly awake. Her nose would not let her return to sleep without some explanation for the odour's source: that, apparently, was the rule.

There was no cumin anywhere within her quarters. It seemed too particular, too smoke-free, too earthy an odour to have emanated from any of the nearby autokitchens; no neighbours, to the best of her knowledge, were hoarders of herbs and spices; and in any case the seal on her door was effectively hermetic. And she'd never known the air circulation, the quality control of which Yolande took considerable pride in, to emit any such aroma. Yet there was definitely an aura of cumin in her room. From where was it coming?

There was only one way to find out.

"Report please, Yolande," she intoned, voice still sleep-slurred. "I can smell cumin." It occurred to her that this was not, in itself, an actionable request to make of the shipmind. She reframed it. "Why can I smell cumin?"

It took several seconds for the screen to activate. Chandrasekhar was not a one for disembodied voices: if she was to speak with someone, then she needed to see a face. That Yolande did not in truth possess a face was of no relevance. The dialogue could only continue once the avatar was instantiated; Yolande knew this, and accepted it, and rose to the challenge with a sense of creativity for which Stef Chandrasekhar supposed the ship's governing intelligence found few other outlets. The screenborne head-and-shoulders simulation which manifested this time was round-faced, dark-hued, curly-haired, kohl-eyed and, from the unconcealed wrinkles and creases, apparently ten to fifteen years senior to Stef herself. Once the avatar *du jour*'s last voxel was in place, the shipmind replied in its trademark distracting contralto: "Is this an existential query, Captain, or an experiential one?"

"It's an I-can-smell-cumin-in-my-quarters-and-I-have-no-bloody-idea-where-it's-coming-from query," Chandrasekhar growled, more snappish and adversarial than she'd intended. It occurred to her that Yolande's chosen visage on this instance was a kind of uncanny-valley echo of someone she had herself known in childhood and had disliked for some now-forgotten reason. She pushed the thought away; rubbed her arms; sniffed again. "That is to say mainly cumin, and a hint of petrichor or rainforest moss, and... something that would like to be garam masala but isn't."

"Are you hungry, Captain?" asked the shipmind, pursing its non-existent mouth in a manner which Stef supposed was intended to simulate kindly concern. "I am given to understand that human dreams sometimes encompass the subject matter of sustenance, digestion, and flavour appreciation, and with your particular sensory—"

"No, Yolande, I was not dreaming about food. I was asleep. A smell, a real smell, here in my room, woke me. Do we have to go through this charade every single time? I would like very much to be asleep again. But I need to know where the smell is coming from."

"My sensors are not detecting any attributable odoriferous activity in your immediate sector, Captain. Is it perhaps some spillage of those components which might have occurred on your garments, during the preceding hours? Something which perhaps went unnoticed at the ti—"

"I'm smelling it *now*, Yolande, it wasn't there before I fell asleep." Chandrasekhar had now remembered just why she'd disliked that girl in school; it didn't improve matters. "And I haven't had anything that culinarily interesting for dinner for the past several daycycles, thanks to the difficulties with food prep which we've been experiencing recently. No, it's not a spillage in my room anywhere. But I can definitely smell it, so it's emanating from somewhere. You're sure you're not detecting anything?"

"Actually, I have been experiencing some difficulties with my sensors lately. There have been a sequence of unexpected failures affecting principally the air quality control monitoring stations," said Yolande. The avatar shrugged its virtual shoulders. "I hasten to add that quality control of the air supply is, in a shipwide sense, secure: there is no identifiable hazardous element present. There have also been, less frequently though often coincident with the locations of the AQC monitoring stations, some as-yet-unexplained failures of audio and holovisual security monitoring. But I—"

"Wait," said Chandrasekhar.

"Waiting," replied Yolande, with the evident patience of the eternal, after several seconds. "Captain, might I ask what I am waiting for?"

"I heard something. Just then. Scratching, in the corridor. Or the vents. It's— no, there it goes again, but fainter now. The smell seems to have ebbed a bit also."

"The monitor for your corridor shows no activity. Nor am I seeing anything untoward in any of the adjacent passageways. Captain, might I suggest—"

"Don't bother," said Chandrasekhar. "Just please remind me, when my duty shift starts, to requisition a report into the sensor failures."

"I can inform Rodriquez of your concerns right now, if you prefer."

"Please don't. He doesn't appreciate other shifts' captains butting in on his command." She said it with a tone of disparagement, though she was well aware that she, on duty, would take it the same way as Rodriquez.

Yolande waited for the customary ten seconds and then asked, "Will that be all, Captain?"

"Yes, Yolande." She dimmed the lighting once more, returned to bed, and hoped sleep would not stay aloof. But her ears now were also on alert, and for all that there was no longer anything to hear, she kept listening out for unexplained noises.

Daycycle 1424

Beatrix thumped the control pad in reckless exasperation, furious at the autoserver's blinkered inability to recognise 'gecko' as a valid foodstuff.

"You have selected (a) gazpacho, (b) gado gado or (c) jello for your meal this afternoon," the autoserver informed her in what had become, thanks to her repeated puncturing of the hapless unit's vox-proc with various of the utensils on offer at the refreshment plinth, a particularly poor imitation of human speech. "Please identify the correct op—"

"Gah! Eh! Seh! Kah! Oh!" she yelled, pummelling the pad for emphasis with each syllable. Belatedly, she thought to look around, but the foodstation was still empty of humans. Besides Beatrix and the current mechanical object of her vexation, its sole occupants were three other autoservers, two of them already vandalised beyond any semblance of utility, one of these quietly leaking smoke.

"Your clarification does not resolve the matter," the unit informed her. "Accordingly, you will be served an equiportionate mixture of options (a), (b), and (c). Please have your meal receptacle ready. This meal will deploy in five, four, th—"

She kicked the reset with her foot. The unit's vox-proc gurgled, and progressed to a continuous, staticky hum. A pungent trickle of grainy red-brown fluid dripped from the autoserver's dispensing chute, then stopped. Beatrix sampled the lukewarm substance, grimaced, then climbed down off the autoserver. It was generally a bad sign when the machines began to smell of ozone.

She ambled across the foodstation's floor and clambered up onto the electronic lap of the sole remaining functional autoserver. She now knew better than to ask for any reasonable form of protein—the machines would not dispense lizards, nor bats, nor slugs, nor insects of any description, instead recommending such outlandishly effete confabulations as 'teriyaki beef', 'lamb consommé', and 'prawn wontons with extra-hot sauce', none of which Beatrix recognised as anything even remotely resembling food.

And, although her spatial memory of the paths to several other foodstations was crystal-clear, the knowledge was of little value if those places' autoservers had not yet been repaired. For all she knew, the machine she was squatting on might well be the last device aboard from which she could get something to eat. With a heavy air of resignation, she gave the instrument a warning kick and intoned three syllables. With a whirr, a 'gloop', and a thud, the machine complied.

Beatrix collected her prize from the autoserver's hatch. Bananas were not, by any means, her preferred fruit, let alone her favourite food, but she had learnt from bitter experience that, on a clarity-of-pronunciation basis, they were the least dangerous choice. She peeled it with her feet and began to eat, complaining to herself that these things never properly filled her up.

Daycycle 1426

There was a wry side to the fact that she had now become a byword—or, more accurately, two bywords—for prodigious versatility and creativity, because she'd long struggled before it was so.

It had taken Kit Warburton years to determine for herself the way she lived best. It was not a mode widely followed. Three square a day just did not work for her, any more than did that strangely entrenched concept of several consecutive hours' sleep. Kit still was uncertain as to whether it was genuinely the case that she was wired differently to most other people, or whether instead the majority adhered, to their own probable detriment, to a daily schedule unreasonably imposed upon them by the strictures of contemporary society, itself needlessly locked in an outmoded planetary rhythm. Her own preferred day length, if such a term could be applied to it, was around ninety-five minutes. A nap; a short stroll around the neighbouring corridors; a solid forty-five minutes, sometimes longer, of creativity; a snack; and, if her metabolism required it, a visit to the smallest room before the next brief nap. Leonardo, she'd understood, had adopted a similar regimen, and, like the Renaissance polymath, her own creative output had burgeoned once she'd allowed herself to fall into this felicitous tempo. It was a pattern equally well suited to creative types and to satellites in low Earth orbit, and therefore largely misunderstood among broader society, since the only other occupations for whom it would ever work were CEOs, mathematicians, and certain categories of prostitute, none of which callings she'd ever felt the pull of.

Her way of being was, in large part, responsible for her decision to have sought a place on the *List of Wealthy Donors*' mission; and insofar as her way of being was the key to her own productivity, it was also what had garnered her that place. Others were here because they were insatiably curious about extraterrestrial intelligence; or if they were not, then because they had evinced that mimicking insatiable ETI-curiosity might yield them subsequent academic fame, funding, and/or superior opportunities for introduction to prospective mates.

Kit Warburton cared nothing much for any of that, except insofar as the exploration of such motivation might conceivably prove suitable material, sometime, for one of her now almost innumerable monographs on what she thought of as Important And Hitherto Neglected Subjects. Her own reason for signing onto the *List* had been the day/night thing. Or, rather, it had been the onboard absence of the day/night thing. It had not been the first such refuge she'd sought during her long and latterly highly productive career. But Svalbard and Antarctica were uncharitably cold, often bleak, and lacking in certain creature comforts, thereby explaining the twinned focus on austerity and refrigeration in much of her early output; and at the other extreme, the thing about cities which never slept, such as London, Shanghai, and New New Delhi was that nightlife, when you analysed it in any sort of detail, was really very irritating and far too strongly redolent of muggings, strobe lighting, fragrant lamppost moats of amphetamine-and-alcohol-infused vomit, inappropriate dance moves, and, struggling to be heard over broadcast dollops of autotuned vocals and dubious syncopation, tinnitus-inducing conversations about sexual incompatibility. The *List* was a godsend: climate-controlled, well equipped, moderately bustling at all hours in case one required an occasional modicum of generally-not-objectionable human company, and largely populated by those who believed 'nightlife' to be a term only applicable to alley cats, bats, moths and the various tribes of the undead, none of which, so far as was known, were aboard. Getting a berth, for Kit, had been a zero-brainer.

She put down her pen, laid her hands palm-down on the desk in front of her, sighed. Allowed her limbic system to experience the mild rush of euphoria which always accompanied a writing project's completion. Then she closed the notebook, stood—a little awkwardly, for arthritis had begun to impose its taxation upon certain of her joints—and gathered up the molehill of well-thumbed reference works for reshelving.

Others thought it odd that Warburton's office was her library was her bedroom, but if they offered an opinion on the matter—which sometimes they did—then they generally qualified it with a supposition that space was at a premium (by which she understood them to mean not the almost limitless stuff through which they were travelling, but the *List*'s incomparably lesser included volume), and that probably it had not been possible to obtain larger quarters. The fact of the matter was that Warburton wasn't bothered in the slightest by her onboard allocation; she liked being able to sleep surrounded by ideas. It served to simplify the task of deciding which ones to write about next.

By rights, it was now time to eat. But she wasn't, at this time, peckish, and the sense of post-project restlessness demanded an outlet. She cast her eyes down at the newly-finished notebook and smiled.

Time, once again, to pay her favourite beta reader a visit.

Daycycle 1428

During the first few months of the voyage, Sal Hinkley retained a sense of slowly-unfolding astonishment at the size of the List of Wealthy Donors. This was not, of course, a particularly uncommon reaction: place a group of several thousand experts in an inherently-convoluted structure of sufficient size to guarantee that most will get lost with almost mechanical regularity, and there will be a significant fraction of those experts who become awestruck, rather than merely disgruntled, at the characteristics of the built environment in which they find (or, on occasion, lose) themselves. But unlike most of the vessel's other occupants, busy with their respective specialisations, Sal took it upon himself to attempt to actively quantify the List's dimensions. He regarded as an oversight the inaccessibility of any detailed blueprints or schematics for the vessel, and as almost an affront Yolande's persistent hesitancy and obfuscation on the subject.

In fact, the List's highly-regarded fabricators had made substantial pre-emptive efforts to smooth over navigational difficulties within the ship's bewildering array of passageways. At launch, the vessel had carried helpful animated smartveneer maps at each of the multitudinous corridor intersections and junctions, helpfully declaring 'You Are Here' in what they believed to be the viewer's preferred idiom, typography, orientation and colour scheme, and pointing the shortest route to the nearest toilets, foodstations, security stations, command centres, health centres, maintenance request points, music venues, jetball practice halls, places of worship and miscellaneous recreational installations. All of this would have been extraordinarily useful and farsighted, except that the revolutionary memorygel adhesive which had been used to affix these maps to the corridors' tile surfaces was not, as it transpired, hyperspace-durable. Many thousands of the useful little smartveneer maps detached from their respective mountings and slid or fluttered or sashayed to the corridor floors. The words 'You Are Here', generally uttered in a mock-plaintive monotone, rapidly became a rather cynical in-joke by which the snarkier of the List's occupants—itself an impressively numerous cohort—greeted each other on their way to find the nearest foodstation, restroom, or amphitheatre. In the daycycles immediately following the unnerving transition into hyperspace, the *List's* senior officers had established a project to replace the fallen and quickly-trampled maps and thereby restore order to the voyage. This project had quickly faltered when the teams sent out had repeatedly become disoriented among the gravity transitions and the multiplicity of near-identical corridor junctions. To compound matters, many maps were stolen by performance artists and redistributed to other shipboard neighbourhoods. Few of the new maps remained intact and in place, and those that did were not trusted by anyone with an assignation, an appointment, or a deadline to keep. Instead, and seemingly at the instigation of Yolande, who Sal presumed to have grown utterly tired of receiving innumerable all-hours requests for shipboard navigational assistance, a fleet of miniaturised pathfinders and route-planners was devised. This was the situation gradually if grudgingly accepted as the new if slightly less convenient normal. But the question remained unanswered: just how big was the *List*?

Sal did not see why the answer to this question could not be straightforwardly answered by Yolande, who surely must know. The shipmind had governance, in effect, over the life-support systems operating across the length and breadth and height of the vessel, which must, therefore, be properties with which she was intimately acquainted. But perhaps it was a body-image matter on Yolande's part, and therefore personal and private; or else (as might indeed be the case) there could be some military secrecy connected to the maximum theoretical size for a hyperspace-going vessel in just the same way that the critical masses of various fissile isotopes had once been forbidden knowledge akin to the names of that Scottish play and of the improbably recurrent villain from that series of books about the boy wizard. Such official clandestinism had apparently been rife in the days before the internet allowed for the ready falsification of anything from celebrity sex tapes to politicians' public misstatements during eminently preventable natural disasters to pipe-bomb design specifications by anyone with a grudge, a modem, and five dollars' worth of freeware. Whatever five dollars' worth of freeware might look like, which was quite another matter.

Hinkley's efforts to satisfy his own curiosity as to the *List's* dimensions through direct measurement were confounded by the ship's design, which doomed to dismal failure all attempts at motion in a straight line over any distance greater than about ten metres. Nor was it possible to know, through any means short of an explicitly-prohibited programme of exploratory drilling, just where were the vessel's outer walls. Following a mishap in which, temporarily blinded by his laser rangefinder, he had almost succeeded in impaling himself with his own self-propelled theodolite, Sal had decided that an intensive volume-estimation programme was more likely to yield useful results than all this hazardous messing about with surveyors' instruments. He began a *de facto* room census of the vessel, estimating the approximate interior volumes of the public spaces with which he was acquainted and seeking to extrapolate beyond that. Over several weekcycles he filled three smartpaper notebooks with his calculations on the dimensions of each room he visited. But rooms aboard the *List* were from time to time repurposed: were Chamber Music Practice Hall 3, Kitespace, and the Junior Bosons' Jetball Training Facility genuinely different spaces within the ship, or were they the same large and unusually-shaped and infallibly *deja-vu*-inducing room, separated by a passage of time rather than by space? Sal could not establish for himself the truth of such matters, one way or another. Finally he opted for extrapolation from his own circumstances. His own personal quarters, which he gathered were unexceptional, had an apparent interior volume of approximately twenty cubic metres; his laboratory was perhaps a hundred cubic metres in all. But his workspace might well be on the large side (for surely a mathematician or a philosopher or a poet did not require as much arbeitsraum as a vertebrate zoologist); an average mission specialist (were there any such beast) might have two thirds or three quarters as much workspace. Say, therefore, that the occupational and personal needs of each person on board necessitated a volume of one hundred cubic metres. But this was *interior* volume, neglecting the walls surrounding it, neglecting also all the infrastructure required to keep an individual fed and hydrated and oxygenated and warm and productively occupied in their chosen pursuit. Say that all these mechanisms and conduits and containers required another hundred cubic metres per person. And then add in another one hundred cubic metres per person for all of the public spaces—because there were a lot of those, and most were rarely crowded. Three hundred cubic metres per person, then. But how many people were on board? Hinkley fancied he'd heard the figure six thousand, but he couldn't be sure whether this was the total population or just the fraction of the population nominally on duty during any of the three recognised shifts. Say ten thousand, then, because it made the mathematics more straightforward.

So, then, a volume of three million cubic metres, which approximated to a sphere of... around one hundred and fifty metres in diameter.

It seemed too small. He had the vague idea that the main jetball arena might indeed be larger than that. Add to this that his quantitation also relied on the kind of slapdash arithmetic which only a cosmologist or an economist could find properly satisfying. His estimate for the volume-cost of each individual might be wildly erroneous, or the assumed occupancy might be wrong, or both. Or perhaps the ship was sixty or eighty-five or ninety-eight percent propulsion system, by volume: all of this was both distinctly plausible and the kind of information which the normally highly-informative Yolande refused to divulge. Sal abandoned his efforts to quantify the List after several fruitless weeks, as more directly work-related matters engaged his attention and his enthusiasm. But he never entirely outgrew the recurrent sense of surprise and awe which would sporadically engulf him, in terms of the List of Wealthy Donors' mesmerising sprawl. He would likely still be finding new aspects to it, and new amenities, ten years into the mission, on the final stages of the voyage home.

Now, on what was for his body clock the evening of daycycle 1428, Sal was walking. He stopped: fittingly enough, at a corridor junction. It was, on this occasion, not disorientation which had caused him to pause, nor the frequent-enough sighting of joggers trotting upside down along the connecting corridor's ostensible ceiling, but the notion that perhaps this, the sense of unknowability that infused the ship's architecture, was what explained Yolande's uncharacteristic reticence to provide detailed structural information about the List. A ship in which there remained 'Here Be Dragons' corners and mysterious, ill-defined connections between domains of local familiarity, a ship too large to be effectively knowable in its entirety, was one in which the occupants were much less likely to experience anything like cabin fever. Could this be the reason? Could the design of the ship itself be a therapeutic attribute, a means of ensuring that those on board, who had no shortage of spaces in which to congregate, could also always find isolation and an opportunity to quietly reflect when that was what they craved? And just like that, Sal Hinkley made his peace with the List of Wealthy Donors' designers and constructors, whom he now saw to be not the Machiavellian debasers of geometric taste and sensibility and starship fabrication that he had heretofore painted them as, but rather a group both far-sighted and wise in the subtleties of human reaction to the built environment.

His reverie completed, he moved on. The poker evening was due to start in less than five minutes. Sal had for some months spent one evening a weekcycle playing poker with Gandel Urkhart, Preston Lavoisier, and Florette Xhang, taking turns to meet in the private quarters of one or other in the group. Fortunately, Sal had made this evening's journey often enough that he was comfortably familiar with the route, and he arrived at Preston's quarters with a couple of minutes to spare.

His host appeared ill-prepared for the card evening, which was par for the course; and significantly flustered, which was not.

"What's up?" asked Sal, the standard pleasantries having been exchanged. His host's quarters looked as though they had been hit by a four-dimensional tornado. So, for that matter, did his host, although given Preston Lavoisier's customary appearance, the error bars on this latter observation were rather large.

"Can you see, anywhere in here, my copy of Kit Warburton's *Effective If Unsporting Techniques In Highly Asymmetric Unarmed Combat?*" Preston asked, furrowing a brow that evidently knew a thing or two about furrowing, and running a distracted hand through where his hair would have been if it was still there. "I put it down somewhere safe, a half-hour or so ago, and now it's vanished."

Sal stared around the other's room, noting the bewildering variety of nooks in which a sufficiently-determined book could conceal itself if it so wished. He sniffed the air. "Have you been eating curry in here?"

"No," replied Preston. "Can't stand the stuff. Can you help me find this book?"

"I'm sure it'll turn up somewhere," said Sal.

"I'm sure it won't." Preston scowled. "Bloody thing's just vanished. Typical."

Sal had learnt, over the past months, not to ask Preston what might be meant by a judgement such as 'typical'. It was simpler that way. He wished the others would turn up: that, too, would be simpler that way. "Get Yolande to replicate you another copy," he suggested, then remembered the promise he'd made to Cyan after last month's disastrous attempt at matchmaking. "But while I remember: you doing anything tomorrow evening? I'm catching up with a friend, and you're welcome to join us."

"What sort of friend?"

"Linguist," said Sal. "She's interesting enough."

*

Fear was quicker; Curiosity stronger. Heart pulsing apace, Beatrix hunkered in the vent shaft, peering in disquiet at the roomful's strange beasts. No two seemed similar, but most, she judged, were carnivores. Some were armoured, others bore feathers, scales or bare skin in fur's place. Several had appendages of an unfamiliar nature and uncertain purpose: perhaps gastronomic, perhaps manipulative, perhaps procreative, perhaps merely decorative.

The beasts didn't move, nor was their smell right.

They weren't alive.

If they weren't alive, they could not harm her. Beatrix inched forward. Curiosity smirked at Fear for being such a big baby.

Fear argued that Curiosity was displaying needless recklessness, but Beatrix had stopped listening. She climbed down from the vent, clambered across to the furred shoulder of the nearest beast. It moved beneath her in a way she wasn't expecting. For a few moments thereafter Fear was all *See? Told you...* but the motion ebbed. Her heart quieted. Curiosity poked its tongue out disrespectfully. Beatrix sought to understand what this place could possibly be.

The room's creatures all hung suspended from high bars, captured in the multitudinous forms of death's grimace. Most were apparently gaffed across the throat.

Trophies? It seemed bizarre; gruesome; crowded. This was a large chamber, comparatively so even by walk-ape standards, but it was made small by having too many of these uncanny hanging carcases.

There was something... *not right* about this macabre collection.

She brushed her hand against the pelt she had landed on. What she touched was not fur, was not a genuine hide. This had never been a living entity. There was no musk, no residue of sweat or blood or excreta; this creature was a sham. Synthetic. Perhaps they all were.

What was the meaning of this place? A host of supposedly-dead creatures, all bipedal, all different, all comparable in size to a two-foot...

She moved across to the shoulder of the next beast, this time anticipating the rocking motion that her weight initiated. She peered inside a mouth brimming with discordant fangs and short tusks. Clambered around the back, ignoring the inanimate touch of an adjacent creature's appendage. The beast's hide was torn—sliced, in fact—down its back, from nape to coccyx.

Beatrix moved further along this row of hanging pelts, clambering from shoulder to shoulder, inspecting the creatures as she went.

All hollow. Soft carapaces. Husks. There was space inside each of these artificial pelts to fit a walk-ape. There were many pelts in this row; and there were numerous rows, ranged across the room.

What was the meaning of this place? What weird purpose did these creature-disguises serve?

She would have to learn more. Curiosity was wide awake.

Her stomach gurgled. She needed a reliable source of protein. But where, and how? Her repeated forays into the vessel's foodstations had become tiresome; and she was beginning to utterly detest bananas.

An idea secreted itself in her brain. It caused a smile. Yes, this was a plan. But could she manage it?

Daycycle 1429

Aboard the *List of Wealthy Donors*, invidious comparisons were drawn not principally on the size of one's living quarters—since it was generally accepted that nobody aboard had sufficient private space—but on their shape, with an intricate theory having propagated which held that room shape was somehow related to onboard social status. Karinette's quarters, which were a kind of gourd shape with a significantly irritating inward dent in one wall, were neither much better nor much worse than most of the others she'd seen (and arguably superior in configuration to Urkhart's own squashed-lozenge lodgings, which might—or might not—put the lie to the social-status hypothesis). Some days, she wondered idly whether the ship's bafflingly chaotic compartmentalisation was the result of collective insanity, or perhaps exceptionally poor drafting skills, on the part of the vessel's design team. Other days, such as now, she merely fumed at her room's obstinate refusal to simultaneously deploy a closet, a full-length mirror, and a washbasin. Any two of them she could access, but not all three at once.

She scrutinised her reflection, frowned, and reached for another outfit. Her foot clipped the edge of the furled mattress, which mewed in soft protest.

"Sorry," she replied automatically, then reminded herself that she'd vowed not to apologise to the furniture. "This one's better, I think," she told herself, holding the three-layer tunic and slacks in front of the mirror.

She was halfway into the tunic when the room's comms hub chimed. "Doctor Lichtermann," she announced.

"Karinette?" asked Urkhart hesitantly, as though after four years there might possibly be revealed another, hitherto unsuspected, Doctor Lichtermann aboard. Granted, the ship was big; but not that big.

"Yes."

"You sound tired."

"I'm not tired," she answered, discovering an involution of some sort in the tunic's fabric and wondering how soon she could get away with terminating the call.

"Because if you are tired, I can jolly well call back, if you'd rather. Would you rather?"

"Frankly, that's not necessary," she replied, with rather more force than she'd meant; and then exhaled, again more sharply than intended. "Honestly. If I was tired, I'd tell you that I was tired. I'm not tired. Really." She pulled the tunic off again and reoriented it: how difficult could it be to find both armholes? "Listen, Gandel, is this urgent?"

"Urgent? No, indeed not. I just thought you might want a heads-up."

"About what?"

"Yolande's dropped a hint or two about tomorrow's practice."

She mouthed a swear-word, hoping it was below threshold for the comms hub's detectors. Was *this* an armhole? It felt promising...

"Are you sure you're not tired? You do sound dashed tired."

"No, Gandel. I'm *not* tired. But I am in a bit of a... What kind of hint? Because frankly, if it's another interpretive-dance-based language fiasco, I fully intend to throw a sickday. On the entirely reasonable grounds that today's walk-through has given me shin splints."

"Uh—no."

"What, then?" She removed the tunic once more and shook it. Maybe it required a full topological analysis. Or a rigorous proof of the Two-Armhole Hypothesis, from first principles.

"It's a combat-based language. Worst-case scenario number 5A."

"Which means what, exactly?" She started to turn the tunic inside out. Or at least, what she hoped was inside out. Why did fashion need to be so complicated?

"Well, don't take this the wrong way... but, depending on how the dialogue goes, I may need to kill you. Purely for emphasis, you understand."

"Gandel? You *do* understand the meaning of the word 'practice'?"

But he'd already terminated the call. *Great.*

She addressed the com-hub again. "Yolande?"

"Good evening, Karinette," replied the shipmind, in her characteristic smooth contralto.

"Anything lethal planned for tomorrow's session? Or has muttonhead—uh, Professor Urkhart—somehow got the wrong end of a completely different stick yet again?"

"I'm not, of course, privy to the intricacies of Professor Urkhart's mental processes. But based on prior experience, it would not greatly surprise me if he has misapprehended some subtle but fundamental aspect of my discussion with him."

"And?" On the sixth or seventh attempt, she had finally mastered the tunic, and was prepared to ignore the possibility that it might be back-to-front, and perhaps even inside out. Hell, at this point she hardly cared if it was upside down, it was *on*. She moved on to the slacks. Slacks were easy. You knew exactly where you were with slacks: no trickery, no ambiguity. Why couldn't tunics be more like slacks?

"I can reassure you," said the shipmind, "that, of course, tomorrow's practice will involve all the usual safeguards, with no significant danger of fatalities. Do you wish me to recontact the Professor, to enquire as to the nature of his confusion?"

"No, Yo, that shouldn't be necessary. He probably just misunderstood 'virtual', or some such. But I do have a suggestion for future briefings."

"Yes, Karinette?"

"If you want to make sure Urkhart understands something, any important directive or what-have-you, translate it into Sumerian, or something equally obscure, before you pass it on to him. Frankly, English doesn't seem to engage his brain in a reliable manner."

"I had presumed that you were going to make a serious suggestion."

"That *was* a serious suggestion, Yo." Where had her closet hidden those shoes?

"I... such a contact protocol is contrary to recommended practice, but I will bear it in mind. Was there anything else, Karinette?"

"No. Thanks, Yo. See you tomorrow."

Five minutes later, having found and then having de-alphabetised her shoe rack, she was passably ready for Sal's habitually punctual arrival. She let the door nictitate open.

"Hi," said Sal from the doorway, running a platonic eye over Karinette's choice of outfit. He was, himself, dressed in a slimming and enviably straightforward combination of jacket, open-collar shirt, and trousers. "You tired, or something?"

"Don't *you* start," warned Karinette. "You ready?"

"I'm here, aren't I?" Sal spread his arms in a shrug of affirmation.

"Then let's go." They set off down the corridor. After a few minutes, and a couple of apparently wrong turnings, Sal beckoned a nav-nymph to guide them to Preston's quarters.

"Thought you knew your way?" Karinette needled her old college friend as the diminutive flying robot took them once again past her own doorway.

"The Meson Scene?" Sal asked.

"Too much a meat market," Karinette replied.

"What about the Zero Gravy?" asked Preston.

"Not at this time of day," said Sal. "More to the point, not at any time of day."

"Airlock Five, then?" suggested Karinette.

"Guess so."

Preston, it had turned out, was overweight, balding, and kaftanned in a garment fashioned from fabric that it would have been kinder to have employed, Karinette thought, in a line of Hawaiian shirts, novelty bow ties, and bandanas. He didn't seem Sal's type at all, and Karinette wasn't therefore sure what, if any, was the relationship between the two of them. Certainly the chemistry between Sal and Preston appeared nonexistent. Nor, on a vessel where one's assigned role in the contact mission pretty largely defined how other people reacted to you, could Karinette gain any kind of appreciation for what Preston actually *did*. He offered no hints on the subject, and effortlessly disarmed the two or three indirect enquiries she attempted. Overall, though demonstrably not shy to share his own opinion, he did not strike her as the kind of person who had any expertise in *anything*; which, on a ship well-and-truly overendowed with experts, made all the more puzzling the fact that this Preston Lavoisier had by a significant degree the most nearly rectilinear, the most fully inhabitable living quarters Karinette had yet encountered in four years aboard the *List of Wealthy Donors*.

Perhaps he was in marketing.

Two beers in, and Karinette was firming on the notion that proximity to Preston was likely to be injurious to one's reasoning ability. The man elevated the *non sequitur* to the status of holy writ. She already felt as though she'd consumed the equivalent of six flagons of Old Hangover.

"It's like cats and dogs, for instance," Preston announced. "I mean, what's *with* that?"

"'With' in what manner?" asked Sal, who, it seemed, was at least trying to pull himself out of the mental quagmire to which Karinette had already ceded all her own cognitive ground.

"With, in the sense of not making sense."

Karinette bit her tongue. In the sense of not making sense, Preston was a contextual fog machine. Mind you, the beer was no help on that score. What she needed, right now, was antibeer. She wondered whether antibeer did indeed exist, and who, if anyone, she might need to kill to get her hands on a supply of it.

"I mean," Preston resumed after a declamatory pause, during which he knocked a small dish of single-cell peanuts to the floor, "cats hate water, right? And dogs love the stuff. Makes no sense whatsoever."

"But—" observed Sal, foot-pushing the peanut dish to be more easily within Preston's reach.

"Because, if you take a sniff, cats don't really smell. Whereas dogs often stink to high heaven. Smelly brutes, dogs. And yet they love getting wet, which generally makes the smell worse, which is surprising, because wetness is the fundamental attribute, the medium I suppose, of the bath, of cleansing. Which cats hate. I mean, you wouldn't credit it."

"I think—" noted Sal, peering down and incrementally repositioning the floored peanut dish for Preston's convenience of retrieval.

"Yeah, I know where you're going. Socialisation. But that doesn't explain it."

"Actually—" said Sal, shifting his stool back from the small table.

"And another thing. D'you actually know what shape a cat is? 'Cause I'll tell you, they're not cat-shaped."

"I don't think—" remarked Sal, reaching down to the floor.

"No, but you'd be wrong," explained Preston. "Not the remotest bit cat-shaped. A few minutes with an electric fur trimmer and a decently thick set of gloves would disabuse anyone of that fallacy. Persians especially. Totally un-cat-like, under all that fur."

Sal, having picked up the peanut dish, now demonstrably free of any hint of peanuts, placed it rather emphatically back upon the table, tilting it as if to highlight its nut-deficient nature to the other man.

"Everybody should try it at least once," said Preston. "Remarkably therapeutic, as well as informative. And pain-free, if you get it right, which admittedly takes a bit of practice. But it's not just the shape. You can learn a lot about things, by examining the cat. The shape's just a distraction. The most intriguing bit—it's all about sex. Look, ever wondered why we can actually *see* cats?"

"To trim their fur, you mean?" Sal asked, evidently mystified.

"We can't," Karinette argued, colouring up as the words even left her lips. Voluntarily staking a verbal claim within this dialogue was, in her view, the conversational equivalent of running into a burning building with a filled jerrycan of hydrazine; and yet, somehow, she could not help herself. "Trim them, or see them. There aren't any cats on board the *List*, I mean. Are there?" She turned to gaze enquiringly at Sal.

"There weren't," Preston said. "Doesn't mean there mightn't be now. Long voyage, large number of scientists with time on their hands, well-appointed labspaces, who knows what they might be getting up to to appease their curiosity? Eh, Hinks?"

"Why are we debating the observability of cats?" Sal asked, after a larger-than-usual sip of his Polar Orbit. "Are you working up some kind of oblique Schrödinger reference, Preston?"

"Who? No, I'm just saying. The reason we can see cats, is sex. That's what it is."

"Isn't that unicorns?" Karinette asked. "At least—"

"Sex?" asked Sal, in the tone of voice normally reserved for critiquing inlaws' wardrobe malfunctions and the most cherished but misguided hypotheses of bitter research rivals. "*Cat* sex?"

"Think about it," Preston implored. And waited, apparently, for them to think about it.

Think about what? wondered Karinette. She was starting to feel decidedly pissed at Sal. The whole point of an evening out was to unwind, to recharge one's mental batteries, to better enable oneself to gird one's metaphysical loins in the face of whatever pseudo-linguistic purgatory Yolande might have ready for her and Urkhart on the morrow. Instead she was of the impression that she was beginning to leak mental battery acid. Cats? Sex? For pity's sake, she could have—in fact, she probably *had* had, on multiple occasions—a more coherent conversation with her mattress.

"If it wasn't for sex, cats would be invisible."

"I'd say—" said Sal.

"No, seriously, I mean, solitary predators and all that. Stalking. Powerful selection pressure, right there. They've had four billion years of evolution to try to make themselves invisible—"

"I don't think—" Sal began.

"—which, after all, is the whole point of the ludicrously OCD cleaning ritual they put themselves through, but they haven't managed the full deal because they need to be able to find each other to breed. Bugger of an obstacle to getting it on, invisibility. Tends to engender a certain skittishness in the party of the second part." Preston sighed at this point, perhaps momentarily overwhelmed by the poignancy of his observation.

Karinette was beginning to feel overwhelmed on other fronts. Such as whether sobriety would be a help, or a hindrance, in this conversation. Consciousness ditto. Perhaps the dialogue could be diverted onto other territory?

But there was, unfortunately, no stopping Preston in full flight of fancy.

"Now, if there was a *really* efficient ambush predator, it'd have bypassed the whole sexual-reproduction glitch, and it'd have mastered the invisibility thing. Its prey would never stand a chance, except by being invisible too, in which case our predator might go hungry. But then—"

"Wait," said Sal. "This is ridiculous! You can't just conflate invisibility with s—"

"Why not? There's plenty of invisible creatures that don't reproduce sexually. When was the last time you saw a bacterium, or a virus?"

"That's size-based, surely," Karinette chipped in, her voice a little more slurred than she'd like. (Against which, it occurred to her that one of the most disconcerting things about Preston was the sheer lucidity of his diction. The man might well be spouting utter bilgewater, but his pronunciation, after putting away an alarming quantity of weapons-grade Martian bourbon, could not be faulted.) "And we *can* see bacteria. With microscopes, at any rate."

"Which is a methodological cheat. You can't expect four billion years of pre-technological evolution to take account of mechanically enhanced optical capabilities."

"And you expect us to believe—"

"Wouldn't have believed it myself," Preston replied, "if I hadn't seen it."

"What *are* you going on about?" asked Sal.

"Well, not *seen* it exactly, because that would be stupid. I mean, claiming to have seen an invisible predator. People would think I was weird, I started suggesting that. Because by definition, essentially, that's a contradiction in terms. Logical inconsistency. So when I say 'seen', I should more rightly say 'indirectly caught sight of indications of,' which is a bit more of a mouthful, but technically more nearly correct."

"What *are* you going on about?"

"Or I could perhaps even say 'amassed visual evidence consistent with the existence of', but—"

"Preston, pardon my French, but what the fuck are you going on about?"

"The invisible predator, of course. Haven't you been listening?"

"Yes, but when you say 'seen'—"

"Perhaps the most correct wording, in deference to our philologically-minded colleague here, would be something along the li—"

"Preston! What do you mean, 'seen'?"

"Well, in a semantic sense, I suppose I should pre—"

"PRESTON!" If it was possible to detonate a word, rather than simply say it, then this is essentially what Sal now did. Several neighbouring conversations ceased, and a plurality of bemused heads turned in Sal's and Preston's direction. An ostensibly off-duty security officer seated at the next table shifted her hand with clearly-practised nonchalance to the craniovoltaic sidearm holstered at her hip. The bar staff appeared interested and momentarily nervous. The air circulators were unexpectedly audible in the aftermath of Sal's interruption.

"On the ship, I mean," said Preston, oblivious to the sudden wider audience. "The invisible predator on the ship. I think I interrupted it in a corridor, and it—"

"Interrupted it how?" asked Karinette.

Sal stood up, abruptly. He was blushing like an apoplectic. "Sorry," he said, *pianissimo*, staring at his wrist-tat. "Just remembered—I left something on in the lab. Better go."

"*Sal*— " Karinette entreated.

"We should do this again sometime," Sal said, in a slightly more audible when-the-reactor-core-freezes-over tone of voice, and hastened for the exit.

"Have you seen the single-cell peanuts?" Preston asked.

Karinette didn't answer. She was staring in futility at her escaping friend, conscious of a rush of envy, discomfort, and despair at what had evolved into a wasted evening. Two horrible, belatedly sobering, and by no means mutually exclusive thoughts had just occurred to her. The less thoroughly unsettling of these thoughts (though not by much) was the belated awareness that, just maybe, she'd been the unwitting victim of Sal's idea of a blind date.

The other thought was distinctly more nebulous, more ill-defined, but received an unpleasant degree of support ten or so minutes later when, on her solitary walk back to where she hoped she might find her quarters, she turned a corner to be afforded a momentary glimpse of something small, furred, and agile, before it reached the sanctuary of the ventilation shaft.

There aren't any cats on board, Karinette reminded herself, the ache in her shins suddenly sharper. She wondered if she hadn't been a little too peremptory in declining Preston's offer of navigational assistance through the *List of Wealthy Donors'* notoriously disarrayed byways.

This wasn't the situation for pathfinding adventurism. Sal lost no time in calling up a nav-nymph and instructing it to guide him to his labspace. Dismissing it on his out-of-breath arrival some few minutes later, he forced himself to count off ten seconds before entering.

He sealed the door behind him. It would be well to ensure that, were there anything awry, it was not immediately relayed to Yolande by the departing nav-nymph.

The office area appeared as it should: a desk littered with smartpaper flimsies; a floor swept largely clear of food wrappings; the control board with that one persistently red light amidst a sea of green and yellow-green telltales. No unpleasant surprises, then. He allowed himself a sigh of what he hoped would turn out to be relief.

He moved through into the cryosuite, was instantly confronted by the unwelcoming chill; but the cryosuite, too, looked to be entirely in order save for that one known and hardly urgent issue. Sal turned, about to leave and lock up, but knew there was that one thing he needed to do, the 'housekeeping matter' he'd been putting off. He'd better dispose of the dead potto in the faulty sleepcasket. After several days the remains were likely to be ripe, to say the least, but there was a breathing apparatus in the office which would serve well enough as a gasmask…

Suitably equipped, he approached the casket, fumbled with thick gloves at the lid, slid it back. Gawked.

Scheiße.

Well. At least now he knew what had happened to his ex-lover's teddybear. He lifted the toy bear out, stared at the empty casket, felt something trickle chill as liquid nitrogen through the ventricles of his heart.

He looked to the cryosuite door, back to the empty casket, and again at the door as though either of those objects held the answer to the myriad questions that were running through his mind.

He'd better do something. The casket had been red-lit for several days; he couldn't properly remember how many. Obviously, he'd need to return the bear to Urkhart, but before that he'd need to raise the alarm with Security. They'd need to do a shipwide search. He left the lab, pacing swiftly down the curved corridor and lamenting his decision to dismiss the nav-nymph.

Better come up with a halfway-decent cover story, though. Something that makes it plain this is simply an accident, nothing more. An escaped animal dangerous by virtue of an infection. Not a human-transmissible infection, though. Nothing more sinister than that.

He paused at the approach to a five-way intersection. What had been that sound above him?

He glanced up, caught sight of the ventilation grille sliding aside, and—

Beatrix moved cautiously forward to inspect the two-feet's body. Hinkley hadn't died easily, and his head was now even more of a bloody mess than was the copy of *Effective If Unsporting Techniques In Highly Asymmetric Unarmed Combat* with which it had been repeatedly bludgeoned (and which now lay beside it); but she had never seen a walk-ape killed before, and she'd had to make sure. Shouldering her synthetic rope and her recently-acquired copy of the versatile and ever-helpful Warburton's *How To Lift Objects Much Heavier Than You Using A Simple But Well-Designed Pulley Mechanism*, the potto climbed nimbly towards the ventilation shaft. Hoisting Hinkley into the shaft, then towing him far enough from the crime scene to reach safety, would not be easy... but if she could manage it, she'd eat well for months. And there was no shortage of other generously-proportioned prey items onboard. She only needed to perfect her attack—probably, she should investigate the other works in Warburton's *oeuvre*, for starters—and she need never worry about hunger again.

Hell, she could even start to think about thawing out Sherman, with whom matters at the time of their recapture and cryosuspension had been left so tantalisingly, so frustratingly incomplete.

Daycycle 1585

The signal was fifty years old. Which meant, as most people accorded such things, that it was significantly older than Karinette. Indeed, it was older than many of the massed experts aboard the *List of Wealthy Donors* who hoped, whether individually or collectively, to overcome the waveform's semantic defences through the raw application of intellect, acuity, logic, guile, distraction, or if nothing else was to hand, dumb luck. Yet such an accounting of the signal's longevity was a singularly anthropocentric view, and quite ungenerous: its accorded span of five decades was merely that which had elapsed, on Earth, since the as-yet-undeciphered signal's first detection as an anomalously semi-regular pattern of radiofrequency peaks originating from the general vicinity of the Galactic centre. For more than a score of millennia preceding their arrival on Earth, the signal's constituent photons had been crawling their way across the Galaxy's vast voids and dust plains, making their slow lightspeed journey across a diffuse, granular and generously illuminated galaxy so enormous that, had it not been merely one of hundreds of billions of such colossi scattered unimaginably far throughout the cosmos, it would have seemed utterly overwhelming in its physical dimensions.

The size of the Universe still managed, on occasion, to confound Dr Karinette Lichtermann. Which was arguably as it should be.

And the signal remained enigmatic. Which was definitely *not* as it should be.

And yet the signal gave Karinette, and so many others around her, a purpose. In a sense the signal was their purpose, just as the sole and complete motivation for the construction and launch of the *List of Wealthy Donors* had been to reach and then to plumb the Galactic region from which the signal had its source. It was a mission for which three distinct generations of unmanned probes had already been dispatched from Earth, in the intervening decades, and had—you will, I trust, pardon the expression—signally failed to yield any results, or indeed to reply in any wise to the anguished tachyonic promptings of their makers and masters.

The signal was aimed at Earth, or at least at Sol system, or at least in a very narrowly-defined direction within which the Sun and its planetary retinue, steadily shunting along in their slow orbit of the Galactic centre of mass, just happened to have lain for the past five decades. Probes sent by hyperspace to Alpha Centauri, to Tau Ceti and to Epsilon Eridani did not receive the transmission; remote beacons at Eris, Sedna and Charon on the solar system's fringes reported its detection but at substantially attenuated strength. The physics of producing so narrowly collimated a beam remained as unfathomable a mystery as the beam's contents, its purpose, and its creators. Fifty years of ongoing reception had failed to dent the signal's inherent internal order, its apparently logical construction, its deeply patterned nature. Karinette had heard just about every conceivable *raison d'être* for the signal. There had been the suggestion that it was a long-duration loop broadcast of the cumulative knowledge of an ancient star-spanning civilisation. There was the hypothesis that it was a form of 'reality radio' soap opera being submitted to the Earth on a trial basis (and associated with which, one presumed, there would be shortly expected to arrive on Earth a high-powered and fearsomely-beweaponed delegation from the home planet of the signal's creators explaining that, should we understandably wish to continue receiving the high-class entertainment which they had for the past few decades been generously lavishing upon us, we need merely part with the entire planetary GDP for the foreseeable future, and perhaps, say, Phobos). Then there was the conjecture that the signal itself might in some manner be sentient, and might somehow constitute a kind of long-duration lightspeed tourist moving in some fashion from distant star system to distant star system, learning of the composition and population of the Galaxy as it did so. A staggering variety of other suggestions had also been posited, generally by those whom one would have considered might well have known better. In fact, the one supposition that Karinette did not believe she had previously encountered regarding the signal's intent was that it might possibly be an extraordinarily complicated, atom-level-detail recipe for the construction of a bowl of blancmange.

"You told Yolande *what?*" she now snapped, as she and Urkhart sat on self-extruding benches in the centre of what was officially the ship's main jetball rink but which was currently serving, for approximately six hours every daycycle, as a training ground for the martial arts classes which had become increasingly popular in the wake of the half-dozen still-unsolved disappearances of personnel that had sporadically followed the apparent demise of Sal Hinkley some five months earlier. It was for just such a self-defence class that they were now waiting: travel time within the *List of Wealthy Donors'* passageways being what they were, those who (like Lichtermann) made a concerted effort towards punctuality were as like as not to find themselves unexpectedly half-an-hour early for any given appointment.

Gandel Urkhart—towards whom the term 'concerted effort towards punctuality' had seldom if ever been applied, except in the form of forlorn plea—placed a distinctly shopworn briefcase on the table between them and looked towards her. He at least had the grace to look sheepish.

"*Blancmange?*" she shrilled, while wondering why it was that the briefcase smelled so strongly of turpentine. "Why?"

"Right. Well. Yes," he began, pausing to remove his spectacles and to wipe the lenses with a handkerchief which, from its appearance, ought really not to be used for any such purpose. "I've been concerned that with Yolande's understandable fixation on the prevalent big-picture family of possible interpretations of the signal's composition, we might by collusion in her training exercises be jolly well blinding ourselves to the possibility that the signal has a distinctly more mundane purpose."

Karinette pursed her lips. It was typical of Gandel, she thought, that he reserved his most formal academic tone for the purest thematic effluent. "Which connects with blancmange," she enquired, "how?"

"It was what occurred to me, off the top of my head."

"Blancmange?" she repeated. "*Really?*"

He nodded.

She fixed him with a stare within which disbelief and disapproval briefly warred before apparently deciding the sightline was sufficiently expansive for them both. "I mean, we're talking about a signal older by all accounts than ninety-nine point five percent of all known human settlements, requiring phoneme-only-knows what manner of resources to transmit across such distances and for such an extended duration, to say nothing of the evident single-mindedness underlying such an endeavour, and you reckon that one possible explanation for this is that, halfway across the Galaxy, some little blue lifeform has suddenly found itself consumed by, utterly convicted by, the notion that, hey, suddenly it's of vital importance to broadcast its progenitor's progenitor's progenitor's blancmange recipe to planet Earth twenty-six-and-a-half thousand light years away?"

"Well. Yes. Indeed so. When you put it like *that*—"

"Do you have any conception of the kind of opprobro— opprobib— public ridicule we, as a shipload of experts would find ourselves in, should you through some utterly freak saving roll on a dozen six-hundred-and-sixty-six-sided dice turn out to actually be correct with such a criminally ludicrous hypothesis? To say nothing of the megacorporations that have funded this jaunt. I mean—"

"It's important that we jolly well not get locked into too deuced rigid a mindset on this," Urkhart responded, steepling his hands. "You've said so yourself."

Her answering glare was as baleful as a blocked combine harvester. It had been a rough day. "What *I'm* astounded at, frankly," she said, "is that Yolande apparently went with it."

"Yes. Indeed so. Well, you know how dashed suggestible she is in these matters. That's the whole bally point of these role-plays, after all, in the sense that they provide for us a forum through which we can just bounce ideas off her, and she enables us to jolly well follow them through to their natural conclusion."

"But *blancmange?*"

"I *like* blancmange," replied Urkhart, as though this could remotely be considered any form of justification. "Which reminds me. Did you request that Yolande communicate all her memos to me in a Persian / Lithuanian / reverse Polish coding of Old Kingdom Egyptian hieroglyphics?"

"No, Gandel, of course not," said Karinette, colouring slightly. "What makes you think I would suggest such a thing?"

"It doesn't matter," replied Urkhart.

"But I *am* pissed at you," said Karinette. "And at Yolande, frankly, while I'm at it, but mostly at *you*. I mean, that's six hours of my life and Heisenberg only knows how many brain cells lost to the thoroughly untenable supposition that the intellects behind the signal are somehow unfathomably fixated upon passing along their Galaxy's-best-recipe for a fluffy white refrigerated dessert. Any more bowls of which, by the by, I frankly do not wish to ever see again, for as long as you live."

"I rather think you mean 'for as long as *I* live'. I mean, 'I' meaning you, not 'I' meaning me."

"I meant what I said."

"I said I'm sorry."

"No, actually, I don't believe you did, until now. So I'm inclined to view your apology with a fairly hefty degree of scepticism." She placed her hands behind her head, stretched, exhaled slowly. "Don't pull that kind of stunt on me again. Ever. Is that clear?"

The martial arts instructor arrived at this point, saving Urkhart from the need for a response.

Sherman had begun his project with high expectations, but with each successive outfit he fashioned for Beatrix, he grew less confident that it would be received positively. The last one, she'd scarcely even bothered to glance at while, hopes ebbing, he'd held it aloft for her perusal. On the available evidence, this one — on which he was, for the first time, trialling tentacles, neoprene, iridescent glitter, and a crest of enticingly downy red feathers — would meet a similar fate. But what else could he do?

He cast his mind back across the past few weekcycles. They'd been turbulent; the arc they made curved undeniably downwards, towards ground and danger.

The revival, his palsying, thaw-racked body coursing with remnants of quick-frozen adrenaline, the legacy of Hinkley's interruption of the inter-species melee in the labspace those several months past. But Hinkley was dead now: Beatrix had shown him the bones.

Those first few glorious hours post-revival: Beatrix had shown the solicitude to let him feed, and to toilet, and then they'd fallen to grooming each other. A universe of two souls. There were other hungers, after all, than those of the belly. They had ravished each other, repeatedly, cocooned within the nest that Beatrix had fashioned for herself, the pile of Hinkley-garments that furnished her ventshaft aerie. The frenzy of it, the marvellous wanton singlemindedness with which they had fallen onto and into and against each other, was something that still coursed through his memories, awakening desire again at each recollection; but those radiant hours had passed. They'd slept, sated, spent, entangled; but when he'd awoken, she'd gone.

And when she'd returned, there'd been a distance, a seriousness about her that he did not know how to breach. He realised that he did not understand her; wasn't always sure she understood herself. This gift, this burden, this complication of intellect was after all a novelty to her, as much as it was to him and to any of their kind, and she alone had had the benefit—or the imposition, if one wished to see it that way—of long weeks apart from anyone else, free to mull it and to contemplate its uses and its meaning. Sherman was not much given to philosophising, did not feel he had to know why something was, or what one ought to do about it; but perhaps this was something more important to Beatrix than it was to him. Sherman knew, after all, why he was awake now: it was because Beatrix had felt the burden of solitude, and had initiated his revival. But neither of them knew what it was that had kindled Beatrix from her long, deep-frozen sleep. Perhaps the unanswered question of that re-emergence into wakefulness— when certainly Hinkley must have been strongly motivated to ensure his murderous little protégés remained inert—was at least a component of her inner uncertainty, her unanchored motivation? For though he did not know what it was which impelled her, plainly there was something doing so.

They still got along, if by 'got along' one meant they still shared food, still groomed each other (a largely pointless relic of innate instinctual behaviour, it had to be said, since there were never any mites or insects on their pelts), still on occasion coupled when the mutual need of it became too pronounced. But there had been something special and substantial between them, those first hours, which now there was not. And it occurred to him, who was not in any sense a strongly thoughtful or introspective young potto, that he missed the thing which had gone, and hoped to reclaim it somehow.

She'd showed him the marvellous hall of walk-ape costumes, some time in that first post-revival week. She'd seemed amused by it; he'd been captivated. Memorised the route; learnt when the chamber was frequented by the walk-apes, and when it was deserted. He'd spend hours in it, at a stretch. If Beatrix noted his fascination with the place, she didn't comment, pursued unknown ends of her own. After a time, just *being* in the room was no longer enough for Sherman. He took trophies.

And after he'd discovered and raided the *List*'s sewing circle's common room, he set about learning how to make costumes for the focus of his adoration.

List of figures included in the illustrated edition of this work

(this is not the illustrated edition of this work)

FIGURE 1: Artist's impression of Corridor 3274-Z aboard the *List of Wealthy Donors*. This corridor has no role of any significance within the present story, and is shown only for context.

FIGURE 2: A potto (*Perodicticus potto*), intellectually unenhanced.

FIGURE 3: Silhouettes, to scale, of (a) a double-decker bus; (b) a blue whale; (c) Belgium; and (d) the Milky Way galaxy.

FIGURE 4: A culinary expert's reconstruction of the noodle dish which Dr Karinette Lichtermann consumed, but did not order, at Crawlspace on Daycycle 186. (*serving suggestion only*)

FIGURE 5: A jetball, disarmed.

FIGURE 6: Wavefunctions depicting the (a) mean, (b) median and (c) modal shape of personal quarters onboard the *List of Wealthy Donors*. A standard human of median gender and ethnicity is also displayed, in silhouette, for context.

FIGURE 7: A nav-nymph.

FIGURE 8: Histogram showing the frequency of production of scholarly monographs by Kit Warburton by year of publication.

FIGURE 9: Figure 8, but in yellow.

FIGURE 10: A bowl of blancmange (terrestrial).

FIGURE 11: Prof. Dr Salvatore Aloysius J Hinkley, in happier times (pre-mortem).

FIGURE 12:   (a) The reptiloid costume which Ensign McGillivray wore in the Language Laboratory sessions of Daycycle 1421 and 1422, in visible light; (b) the same costume, in ultraviolet light, with synthetic protein stains and perspiration marks highlighted.

FIGURE 13:   Audiogram of a randomly-selected segment of the Galactic-Centre-origin radio transmission. The segment depicted is of approximately five minutes duration.

FIGURE 14:   A skyline transect showing, in silhouette, approximately ten kilometres of alpine ridge, scanning due west from the Matterhorn. The similarity to the audiogram shown in Fig. 13 is striking, but is believed not to be significant.

FIGURE 15:   An artist's impression of the hypothetical exoplanet on which the signal-sending race might hypothetically dwell, commissioned by the *List of Wealthy Donors'* construction consortium before launch and included here because such things always help a book sell.

FIGURE 16:   (a) A typical banana (Cavendish) produced by a functioning autoserver; (b) a functionally equivalent item produced by a badly-damaged autoserver. Though the gross nutritional values of the two items are almost identical, clear differences are evident in aesthetic properties and structural stability.

FIGURE 17:   Preston Lavoisier, undated, photographer unknown. The image's similarity to a police mugshot is thought to be coincidental.

FIGURE 18:   A pair of bifocal spectacles, grimed and dirt-encrusted. These spectacles, believed to be the property of Prof. Gandel Urkhart, were found discarded in the *List of Wealthy Donors'* language laboratory on or around Daycycle 1642, and remain unclaimed.

6

Daycycle 1643

The stroll was at once a marker of achievement—another title completed—and an opportunity to recharge the batteries of inspiration. Viewed differently, it was a *cordon sanitaire* with which to seal off the old work-in-progress and to allow Warburton to assess the relative merits of competing prospective projects before embarking on whichever topic she next decided on. It was a very freeing, mentally profitable sensation, to know that she was currently at liberty to allow her mind to wander wherever it would: writing, especially her variant on the task, required a degree of singleminded fixation, and its occasional absence brought welcome relief.

The route she took was a familiar one. It was well not to distract the mind, at a time like this, with a need for conscious navigational consideration. She knew these particular physics-graffiti-daubed, grimed, grav-tiled byways like the back of her hand. For most people, such an assertion would be idle metaphor; but Warburton had done the maths. Median albedo 0.68; mean corridor radius 1.35 metres; apparent local gradient 0.06; mean coefficient of friction for moccasins on tile 0.15; nineteen hundred and seventy-five standard Warburtonian strides, all up. Sometimes on her walks she met people, on occasion even people she knew, as they were leaving the autokitchen or the entertainment hall or the nondenominational place of worship. Today it was quiet: she'd sighted only a maintenance trolleybot and a pair of security officers embroiled in some sort of mid-corridor discussion that had actually been quite awkward to detour around, the corridor being inconveniently narrow at that point. At the closest approach, the rustle of cloth against cloth had been unavoidable, the sensation of personal-space intrusion unfortunate. She turned the second-to-last corner—

Stopped, so as to avoid stumbling on the fallen ventilation grille. Stared at it, glanced up. Could not immediately categorise what she saw, had barely time to register *feathers* and *tentacles* and *steak-knife-loaded machine crossbow* and *I would seem to have overlooked an option in my tome on the application of kitchenware to weaponry* and—

There was a flash of movement. Three quick-spaced thunderbolts embedded themselves deep in her ribcage. And suddenly it was all a bit too acutely painful and desperate and then a bit irrelevant and numb and rather too late.

There would be no more words.

"Six bamboo," said Melia, placing the tile down.

Karinette picked up from the wall, contemplated her own row of tiles, and reluctantly played one she suspected she'd regret, because that was how it usually went. It didn't matter too much. She hadn't joined the mahjong circle out of any sort of competitive spirit, and indeed it wasn't that sort of mahjong: not pure, not classic, not entirely one of the bastardised Western versions either. Mostly it was an opportunity to unwind, to stave off both ennui and stress amidst a group of still mostly strangers. Not for her the seismically deafening and saccade-inducing charms of jetball that so captivated such a large fraction of the *List of Wealthy Donors'* ostensibly insular and seemingly serious-minded personnel with its flashily ballistic penalty shootouts, its thumping gravity-switch tackles, its crowd-deafening cyberthrash crescendos accompanying even the least-accomplished scoring shots, its propulsively percussive offensive play; Karinette very much preferred a pastime where one didn't have to be unduly concerned about polymer fatigue in one's blastproof exoskeletal team kit or spectator shield. (And if and when they met the signal's transmitting race, how would they even explain the inexplicable concept of jetball to them, and would such explanation constitute an inadvertent declaration of interspecies war?) No, a quieter mode of recreational expression was more in keeping with her sensibilities. But baking didn't appeal; she had no defensible musical talent (as close friends had attested on several occasions—mostly those involving alcoholic refreshment—when she had attempted to demonstrate otherwise); she categorically refused to stoop to one of the shipboard life-drawing circles, either as model or artist; and improv would have been far too much like her day job for purposes of effective relaxation. Mahjong didn't properly fill the gap that had been left in her life by Sal's death, but once she'd realised it was unfair to expect that of the activity, she'd begun to enjoy it. She'd felt guilty about that, to begin with; but what else could she do?

Tiles were harvested from the wall; tiles were sown into the centre. As play progressed, interspersed with a rambling and multi-stranded conversation between the table's four players, Karinette began to feel that she was getting close to a victory. Then Cyan called "Mahjong" with a broad smile and a soft yet unmistakeable flourish of satisfaction, and displayed her winning hand. The others complimented her on it. Then all four hands were tipped into the centre.

"Another round?" Hamdi asked, watching the pseudo-aware tiles turn themselves face-down and redistribute themselves.

"May as well," said Melia Pernillesdottir, who seemed, as usual, by some personal alchemy (the wellspring of which Karinette could never satisfactorily fathom) to have appointed herself the *de facto* role of table leader. The tiles set about reconstructing the game's four walls.

"You still seeing that jetball heavy?" Cyan asked.

"She's not a heavy," Hamdi protested, without lifting his eyes from the tabletop.

"Guess that answers that question," said Cyan. "So things are getting serious?"

"Cyan!" Melia reproached. "You're so nosy sometimes."

"No, I wouldn't say they were serious," said Hamdi, straightening the two-high row of tiles in front of him.

"Ah," said Cyan, knowledgeably. "Friends with benefits?"

"Cyan!" exclaimed Melia.

"More frenemies with complications," Hamdi mumbled.

"When you say fren—"

But Hamdi had evidently decided that the conversation required diverting. "It hits me every so often," he began, voice several decibels higher than before, "just how crazy this all is."

"Sexual relationships?" Cyan asked.

"Inquisition?" asked Melia.

"Mahjong?" Karinette asked.

"No," he replied, gesturing around the room, at the five or six tables occupied by other players. "This. The voyage. A signal that remains undecipherable, and an alien race about whom we know nothing, not even the fact of their continuing existence."

"No shop talk," warned Melia, rolling the dice.

"It's not shop talk," replied Hamdi, stroking an emaciated moustache which Karinette always felt should simply be put out of its misery.

"We none of us work together, so there's no 'shop'. So it can't possibly be shop talk."

"If you're talking about the mission, it's shop talk," said Melia. "We're all involved. Who's East Wind?"

"You are," said Cyan. "You just rolled."

"What'd I roll?" Melia asked.

Oh, for pity's sake, Karinette thought. *The dice are right in front of you.* "Five." Melia counted off along her section of wall.

"It makes no sense that the signal would target Earth," said Hamdi.

"Whyever not?" Melia asked. "We're an intelligent, technologically advanced civilisation. It stands to reason, I would say, that a likeminded civilisation would seek to initiate contact with us, to ensure it carried the initial momentum in the unfolding interaction."

"We don't even know if it *is* a likeminded civilisation," argued Karinette. "We can only guess at its mindedness, like or unlike. We don't know the first thing, really, about whoever is sending us the signal."

"I don't even mean that," said Hamdi. "What I mean is, the signal is thirty thousand years old. Thirty thousand years ago, we probably didn't even have language."

"Twenty-six thousand," said Melia.

"We had language," Karinette said. "Language is older than most people realise." She strove to suppress, as uncharitable, the thought that *shouldn't a historian, of all people, know such a thing?* But she suspected that Hamdi, who with Urkhart had enjoyed some sort of pop-culture vogue, as surprising as it was brief, with their collection *Bawdy Limericks of the Egyptian Middle Kingdom* (followed by the distinctly-less-successful *Haikus of the Etruscans* and the seemingly-unpublishable *Clerihews of the Hittites*), was as a scholar of the written word somewhat blinkered about aspects of his field beyond his particular specialisation. (It might, she mused, explain how he had managed to collaborate creatively with Urkhart, whom she had long felt to epitomise such blinkeredness...)

"Okay," he conceded. "But I'm right, aren't I, that the signal is thirty thousand years old?" He looked expectantly towards Melia.

The engineer sighed. "Twenty-six thousand. And I'm not sure why you're choosing to kvetch about that just now, after almost five years aboard. We'll have reached the target in another six monthcycles; we'll know soon enough."

"If anyone's still there," said Cyan.

*

53

Captain (Third Shift) Chandrasekhar preferred not to use the direct route from her quarters to the bridge. The way was conveniently short, but it led past two erratically-maintained autokitchens, a mixed-gender jetball locker room, and an organic waste storage depot, any of which could be fairly reliably expected to prove nasally memorable to someone of her sensitivities. A simple detour obviated exposure to the depot and the more generally problematic of the autokitchens, but took her past a connecting corridor leading to a chamber she had long suspected, on the available evidence, of housing some kind of twenty-four-hour R&D facility for synthetic bog butter and artificial fish entrails. Consequently, she had been experimenting almost from day one with progressively more didactic, but less odour-exposed, approaches to the task of getting from A to B. So what if it required three kilometres of careful navigation to cover a span, as the neutrino flew, of less than fifty metres? The walk was enjoyable, if one told oneself that this was what enjoyment felt like. And even a starship captain (third shift) needed exercise.

She turned a fresh corridor. This one seemed promising. The best passageways, she'd long since decided, were those that led neither through the List's industrial bowels nor its residential ventricles. The corridors lined with storage facilities or with seldom-frequented meeting chambers tended to be somewhat stale-smelling, but generally no worse than that. It was irritating that such stretches generally did not directly connect with each other, but through trial and error she was usually able to find a way to minimise the discomfort of any interlude between them. Here, with a long storeroom for medical-grade towelling and plastilinen bedding to her left and a series of almost-invariably-deserted interview rooms on her right, the corridor was not completely odour-free, but it was at least pleasantly bland. She needed merely to decide whether to cut once more through the entertainment precinct after the next-but-one intersection, or whether a dive through the adjacent residential corridor—which on her last pass had carried painfully vivid memories of sauerkraut—might not lead to an overall better route.

She was aware that most of her fellow crewmembers would have found her peregrinations unnecessarily circuitous; inefficient; perhaps borderline compulsive. She didn't care what other people felt. In a difference of opinion between her nose and a dozen arbitrary colleagues, she'd trust her nose every time. She was, all up, quite the nasal iconoclast.

It had always been thus, she reflected as she reached the next junction, her subconscious making the decision for her. The reliance she placed on scent hadn't done wonders, in earlier years when she could be bothered about such matters, for her love life. It turned out that the men and women who smelled the most alluring were not always what they seemed. She dreaded to think how many times her nasal acuity had led her astray, had interfered in the search for romance or nocturnal adventure, or had simply got in the way at a sensitive moment. Her habit of reeling off, verbatim, a prospective partner's moment-by-moment olfactory 'tells' had sometimes proven problematic: she remembered one lover, in college, who had memorably complained to her that it was like kissing a mass spectrometer. She'd learnt, after that, to keep such aromatic disclosures to herself; had tried to place less emphasis on airborne molecular signals in forming judgements on people she met. But it was hard to have complete respect for someone who didn't smell the way they ought. So she'd given up on that side of things, the romantically interpersonal, quite early. Perhaps it had been this, as much as anything, which had driven her towards the career she'd chosen. She'd had to work damned hard—as anybody would, unless they had simply been born with the right connections, like Styring or Jespersen—to achieve a position from which she could keep others at a sufficient distance to not be overly distracted by the combined scents of urine drizzle and odour nullifier on a trouser leg, or by the burnt-coffee aura which habitually seemed to accompany the strongly motivated, or by that fresh, too-strong smell of soap which always made her suspicious about a person...

It was a matter of sensitivity. But call it 'sensitivity' and people make you, in their minds, into something effete, and delicate, and by implication impeded in some social or behavioural sense, and she refused to see herself in those terms. She was simply determined to do things her way, and if others thought her quirky or in some fashion confined by the characteristics she'd been born with, that was their problem, not hers. She was broadly content with the person she'd become. It could not be denied, however, that her nose sometimes still led her astray, as it had done on this morning's walk. Thus it was that she found herself lost, on this particular morning, faced with an unfamiliar six-way intersection and only five minutes until commencement of her shift. She knew Rodriquez would fill in for her—he would be only too eager to do so—but she was damned if she was going to give him the satisfaction of seeing her turn up even one minute late to relieve him.

She stared along, down, and up each of the corridors in turn, and sniffed. Amidst the multiplicity of background scent-strands—perspiration, citrus, ozone, disinfectant, cooking oil, mould, grease, a hydroponics chamber, her own carefully-minimised perfume—she caught the faintest whiff of hot buttered fishguts. Reoriented. Checked again. Smiled. She had her bearings now. It didn't matter that she didn't recognise the corridor itself, she knew it led to a sector with which her nose, at least, was familiar. She strode, pivoted as the grav-tiles switched wall to floor and vice versa, dodged a lost-looking unicyclist, turned to the right at the next intersection. All she needed to do now was to take—

Suddenly, lateness for the start of her duty cycle was the least of her problems. She knew it well before she reached the crucial junction. The smell of death was pungent, unmistakeable.

"If anyone's still there," Melia echoed, suppressing a yawn. "And if it doesn't turn out to have some bizarre but natural explanation, like an unnecessarily complicated pulsar or something. But, yes, so far as we can determine, the signal is co-located with a small main-sequence star approximately one hundred and fifteen light-years shy of Sag Bee Two, which means it's taken twenty-six thousand three hundred years to reach us."

"That doesn't strike you as odd?" Hamdi asked. "That level of precognition? I mean, that they'd single out an apparently-insignificant solar system so far out from their neighbourhood, and start signalling it at a time when its most intellectual inhabitants were squaring it off with bears and sabretooths for the dubious privilege of cave ownership? I mean, how did they even know Earth sustained a technology-capable species, back then?"

"Maybe they didn't," said Karinette. "The transmission might be entirely inadvertent. Interstellar butt dial."

"Disaster for the mission, if true," said Cyan. "Though at least we'd learn they had butts."

"Clearly they'd visited," Melia told Hamdi, counting along the wall of mahjong tiles once again, then pausing. "I've always suspected they must have hyperflight. It'd only be a matter of time before a technologically advanced race like that mapped the entire galaxy. They may well be keeping tabs on dozens of other planets bearing advanced lifeforms. Just because the signal is apparently aimed directly at Earth, and Earth alone, doesn't mean they mightn't be also transmitting other signals to other planets. Just on the off chance, as it were."

"But if they have hyperflight, why are they using a slow lightspeed technology like radio transmission? Why not drop a probe right into the solar system and broadcast from that? You're arguing they have that technology, which seems plausible enough—why aren't they using it for the signal?"

"Perhaps they're shy," Cyan ventured. "Besides which, we don't even know if they're genuinely trying to say anything. I mean, it might be the alien equivalent of, I don't know, a twelve-bell peal or a prog rock synth solo or something. Noise, with a readily apparent structure but with no real informational content."

"Frankly, though, even if it's just structured noise," said Karinette, "that at least still indicates the presence of a consciousness with some understanding of the principles behind that imposed order. It's still a demonstration of intelligent thought on some level. You can't have a highly-structured narrowcast that isn't, ultimately, the product of intellect, and therefore of meaning."

"You've never worked in advertising, have you?" asked Cyan.

"You're all missing my point," said Hamdi, running an aggravated hand through what remained of his hair. "The signal happens to have arrived at the very point in our history when, for the first time, we could actually do something about it. It only reached Earth five decades ago, well into the era of spaceflight and quantum computing and that mercifully shortlived fad before the copyright laws caught up with celebrity-lookalike gene therapy. But it started sending thirty— I mean, *twenty-six thousand odd years ago*. Before we had the telegraph, the oxcart, the safety match. Doesn't that all strike you as ever so slightly freaky?"

Dread pierced his core in that instant. Walk-ape footfalls, heavy, nearing. Sherman jerked his hands free of the disarrayed rope. Twisted awkwardly in the loose-fitting costume.

The urge to flee surged within him.

The vent. The crossbow. The human. The dropped book. The lack of time. He tripped over his own costume's tentacles, grabbed the nearest item. Then the rope. Climbed.

Haste. Grip uncertain. Hands a-slip. No time. Haven ventshaft. Relief.

Panting. Heart thundering. Haul the rope. Don't leave clues.

But he'd left the crossbow, and the knives.

Too late now.

Cries of walk-ape shock. The alarm's clamour.

Sherman edged back from the lip of the ventshaft opening. Then gathered up rope, winch, and book. Set off towards the nest of his home with Beatrix.

The smell of failure. He was angry at Beatrix in that moment: her insistence that he step up, make a kill. Fresh meat. She should have known he wasn't equal to the assignment. He lacked her ruthlessness, her edge, her fearless determination; could offer only pretence. Beatrix might have the stomach for big-game hunting; he, plainly, did not.

He was angry at her; furious with himself. He'd managed the kill, but had fumbled all else. So what if he had been interrupted in the task of carcass retrieval? He had been armed with an evidently lethal firearm, had needed merely to reload. But there hadn't been time. She'd know that for the feeble excuse it was. He hadn't even tried to prise the knives loose from the human's ribcage; instead, he had simply panicked and fled.

It had been a major mistake to agree to her suggestion. He had only done so because he had thought she might like him more, once he returned with food. Wished to prove himself adult male potto enough. Which he wasn't. So she wouldn't.

The winch, snarled with hastily-collected cord, was awkward to carry. He discarded it at the next intersection, hoping it was far enough from the site of his botched killing to escape detection should the walk-apes try to search the narrow vent shafts.

He'd hoped to impress her; but that, now, seemed more distant than ever. It would be bananas, again, for dinner, and she would not be pleased.

He tripped at the next turning, landing with a small thud that the costume didn't entirely cushion. He was still carrying the useless, bulky book that the useless, bulky two-foot had dropped. He considered leaving it. As a trophy, it was not likely to impress Beatrix, who would comment sharply on its lack of edibility. But no, he wouldn't, because it was *proof*. Proof that he hadn't chickened out.

Except, of course, that he had.

And maybe it would turn out that the book was recipes, ways in which an experienced hunter like Beatrix could render her prey even more delicious?

Yes, he decided as he laboured through the long series of ventshafts, that was how he'd present it to her. He'd find some way to encourage her to find some positive in his return, encumbered not by fresh meat, nor by her carefully-fashioned crossbow, but by a book.

On such small—and, it has to be said, ill-judged—decisions does history turn.

"Coincidences do happen," said Cyan. "Maybe that's when the signal-sending race first developed the technology for it."

"In which case, why signal Earth?" Hamdi asked.

"Maybe they'd detected Earth as one of the few planets across the Galaxy with abundant life, and decided to signal on the off chance. They don't have to have visited us. We don't yet know what it is we don't know."

"We'll know in six months," replied Melia, picking up the dice. "Who's East Wind?"

"You are," said Cyan. "You already rolled."

"What did I roll?"

"My eyes," said Cyan.

"Six," said Karinette. A sense of dismay had begun to worm its way through the casing of her wellbeing. Not so much at Hamdi's eleventh-hour second thoughts regarding the signal's pedigree, nor at Melia Pernillesdottir's uncharacteristic distractedness; rather, what was bothering her was the realisation that the complexities of mahjong were sufficient to enable Yolande to perceive it as a possible substrate for language, and therefore for workshopping in the lang lab. The value of mahjong to Karinette was largely that it served as an escape from the tedium and strain and confusion of her daily sessions with Yolande and Gandel; she didn't want that avenue of escape tarnished. Appropriated. Fed into the melting pot.

Still, as Melia observed, there were only six months until their arrival in the target system. Maybe Karinette's luck would hold...

On a tangentially-related note, Sherman got lucky that daycycle, though not in the manner he'd hoped for.

The same could be said, also, of Beatrix.

Others aboard? Less so.

7

Sal Hinkley's death weighed more heavily on the circuitry which contained Yolande's conscience than did any of the half-dozen other as-yet-unsolved deaths that had succeeded it. Not that the shipmind was in any way directly involved in Hinkley's loss, nor in any of the subsequent tragedies; but she nonetheless felt keenly that it was a demonstrable failure of care, of stewardship, of vigilance on her part to have even unwittingly allowed his death by an as-yet-still-unidentified assailant. Hinkley had had no warning of his end; a situation which, in all likelihood, also held for those slain after him, but at least they had been aware of the shipboard precedent, aware on some level that nothing on the *List of Wealthy Donors* could guarantee the safety of someone walking its corridors alone.

It irked Yolande, too—though she would never have thought to give active voice to such an opinion—that the public grief on board appeared to be invested most heavily in the memory of the most recent victim, the astonishingly-prolific Kit Warburton, whose works such as *Improvising Vacuum-Safe Spacesuit Repairs With That Boysenberry-Flavoured Gelatine Powder You'd Forgotten You'd Left In The Sample Pouch* and *More Barbecuing With Cyclotrons: Forty New Mouthwatering Strange-Matter Recipes That'll Delight Your Crewmates* and *Bring A Safety Pin To A Knife Fight And Emerge Victorious In Three Easy Steps* were seemingly to be found on the bookshelves of just about every mission specialist on board. Yolande conceded that Warburton's contribution to the world of nonfiction literature was unprecedented, but she nonetheless felt that the sense of loss exhibited in Warburton's direction was disproportionate, and disrespectful towards the other victims. Was not the worth of a human something to be assessed by measures other than that individual's output? Did not each person carry their own intrinsic worth, independent of all external considerations? Were not all of them equally deserving of grief, and of remembrance? Her programming held that it was so.

This is not to say that Yolande was entirely preoccupied by Hinkley's demise, nor indeed by the others. Regret did not equate with fixation. Her concerns, such as they were, ran in parallel to the continual monitoring of the controlled nuclear reaction which maintained the *List of Wealthy Donors'* precarious grip on the metafluid surfaces of hyperspace; to the processing of routine maintenance orders for an air-circulation system that had been struggling, of late, with unexpected odours and interruptions of supply; to timekeeping, at the one-thousand-and-twenty-four-bit accuracy required for successful tachyonic astrogation; to participation in, at this instant, two hundred and thirty-seven simultaneous games of chess, Go, or five-dimensional Texas hold 'em with off-duty researchers; to the three thousand or so work-based or recreational conversations in which she was currently involved, on topics as diverse as superheavy-element stabilisation within a strong magnetic field, pictorial evidence for the existence of inhabited two-dimensional domains within ancient Egypt, and whether tardigrades have any awareness of the concept of natural justice; and to the optimal approach to take for autokitchen repair and upkeep during the monthcycles ahead. The pain which Yolande felt at Hinkley's continuing absence—and it was pain, for he had been an interesting conversationalist, when he set his mind to it, with a keen appreciation for the strengths and limitations of artificial intelligence—was different in many respects to that which a human would have felt. But the pain was no less genuine, no less deep, for all that. It was precise, it was efficient, it was enduring. It was compounded, too, by the apparent rapidity with which so many biologicals moved on, despite their notoriously sluggish clock speeds, from a sense of loss; as though it all simply ceased to matter.

Hinkley was dead. Simcic was dead. As were Gamble, Kristianson, Davies, Suzuki, and Warburton. There was nothing Yolande could do to bring them back, yet she would persist in holding their memories within hers, and to ensure they did not fade in remembrance. It was something which the humans apparently would not, or could not, do.

Biologicals were so difficult to understand sometimes, both individually and *en masse.*

Daycycle 1660

"Lavoisier?"

The voice was female, a bit tired, a bit Transatlantic, more than a bit not inclined to put up with any bullshit—it was impressive, really, how much additional information could be packed into just three or four syllables—and reached him from uncomfortably close by. Preston looked up from his doodling, turned around enough to take in the woman who owned the voice, answered "Yes" in exactly that tone of voice that means "No", and sank inwardly, though the last was probably disguised fairly effectively by the kaftan. He got up from the bench in the sad little shipboard park, caught his elbow on the nearest branch of the nearest sad little shipboard tree, and asked "How can I help you?" in exactly that tone of voice that means "Please go away", because although he had never seen this woman before and although she had turned up almost eight months after the fact, he knew exactly—from those same three or four prefatory syllables, and from her crew overalls—just what it was she wished to talk with him about, and he did not wish it.

He could not say that, of course, because to say that would be interpreted as an admission of guilt. Not that it was. But he would have to say something which would minimise the damage, nonetheless.

"Adrienne Christofforou-Takahashi," she informed him, offering a dangerous-looking hand which he shook with substantial reluctance. "Security."

"Is the park closed?" he asked, looking around himself at the sad little park. *If nothing else is on offer, attempt levity.*

"Nothing like that," she said, taking her seat on the bench and indicating he should do likewise. He did so, maintaining as great a distance from her as was nonetheless permitted according to the principles of Euclidean geometry as they applied to this particular item of supposedly-outdoor furniture. "I was hoping we could have a few words. About Dr Hinkley, and the eveningcycle on which he went missing. Fourteen twenty-nine. Can you cast your mind back to then, provide me such details as you can recall of the circumstances as you are aware of them?"

"Isn't this rather late in the piece to be raising this? I mean, Sal vanished quite a long time ago."

"We've been stretched," said the woman from Security, and her voice made it sound as though some such skeletomechanical process may indeed have occurred, even if it appeared, in her case, not to have taken. "There has been a lot of vandalism to deal with—"

"Which surely shouldn't take priority over investigation of something which might yet turn out to be murder."

"You might say that, but when so much of the vandalism is centred on the food-fabrication devices needed to keep the shipboard population alive and active, it's not so black and white. Ensuring the continued wellbeing of the many becomes the more urgent task. Plus there have been several additional capital crimes, plus we in Security were for several monthcycles working under the misapprehension that Hinkley was a high-energy particle physicist rather than a"—she glanced down to check something which seemed to be insta-tattooed on her palm—"comparative vertebrate neurobiologist—"

Preston turned so as to better remonstrate, nearly falling from the bench in the process. "You say that as though his occupation makes a difference to whether you investigate the disappearance."

"It does, actually," Officer Christofforou-Takahashi said. "Disappearances of high-energy particle physicists, on a vessel travelling full pelt through hyperspace, are usually self-inflicted misadventure, so far as we in Security have been able to ascertain from the four which have occurred since the start of the voyage. We'll likely never know exactly what happened to them, and after Guilfer's disintegration we've been banned by Chief Thacker from attempting any more reenactments... but Hinkley wouldn't have been involved in anything occupationally hazardous like that, he just worked with animals, so his disappearance is quite out of character."

"And you want me to tell you what I know?" Preston asked.

"That we do," she said.

"It's not much," he said, a claim he then went on to substantiate.

"We're using the wrong dashed 'they'," said Urkhart, pausing in the act of loading the paintball bazooka.

"Gandel, there is no other 'they'," replied Karinette, wiping blue gunk off her goggles, an action which largely made it worse. McGillivray was visible only as a smudge on the edge of her vision. From the smudge's motion, it appeared the ensign was reloading. Karinette tried to assess which of the nearby shapes might provide cover. "They're a hivemind, 'they' has to be plural."

"Yes, but there'll jolly well be two forms of the plural. One for a self-aware collective, and one for a grouping where the threshold for sentience hasn't been reached."

"Then there'd also be two forms of first person and second person— okay, wait, maybe there wouldn't be," said Karinette, ducking low enough that their counterpart's next question splattered harmlessly on the lang lab wall behind her. "D'you think we've offended them?"

*

"So that's all you're able to recall?" Christofforou-Takahashi asked, five minutes later.

"Yes," said Preston.

"Did you notice anything, anything at all, which might be seen to be unusual or out of character about Dr Hinkley's behaviour during your evening out?"

"He knocked over a dish of single-cell peanuts, if that's what you mean," said Preston. "I mean, he didn't do that often."

"I see. That wasn't really what I meant. Well, I'm afraid none of this gives us particularly much to be going on with. Just one final thing: we'll need your occupation for the formwork, but at this stage we don't seem to have it."

"That's unfortunate."

"It's odd that Yolande has no record of it."

"Does she not? That rather surprises me."

"It certainly surprised us."

"I suppose it would," said Preston.

"Do you mind telling me what it is that you do aboard, Mr Lavoisier?"

He resisted the impulse to glance away, knowing that Yolande would be cognisant of this conversation as she was of almost everything else which occurred onboard the *List of Wealthy Donors*. He thought quickly. "I'm an evangelist," he said quietly after several seconds, splaying his palms outward as though this were any kind of explanation, in any kind of language, of what an evangelist was or did.

"Oh yes," Christofforou-Takahashi replied with wary courtesy. "What kind?"

"Male, middle-aged, mildly overweight. Apparently very good in b—"

"No, I mean what's your... denomination, or whatever it is they call it?"

"Ussherist."

"Eucharist?"

"Ussherist. We're not many, these days. You likely haven't heard of us."

"No, I don't believe I have. Can you tell me a bit about it?"

"Is it relevant?" Lavoisier asked. "To Sal Hinkley's disappearance, I mean."

"Probably not," said Christofforou-Takahashi. "But I'm interested nonetheless."

Damn, thought Preston. "Well. Have you heard of Bishop Ussher?"

"Can't say I have. Is he or she onboard?"

"He. No. Died several centuries ago. But he determined the precise age of the Universe."

"About fourteen billion years, isn't it?"

"Oh, no no no. No. Much younger. Just a bit over six thousand years. It started back in October the somethingth, 4004 BC."

"But there's a wealth of scientific evidence—" said Christofforou-Takahashi.

"That it's much older, yes. That's the way it seems. But the Ussherist view is that all of this so-called evidence nonetheless was formed back in 4004 BC, as a test of faith, or possibly a divine prank, or both."

"I'm not sure I—"

"The creed has a particular resonance with our mission onboard the *List of Wealthy Donors*. None of us know what we're heading into."

"That's true enough, yes," said Christofforou-Takahashi. "You mean we don't know who sent the signal, nor what it says?"

"More than that," said Preston, warming to his hastily-conceived spiel. "We don't even know anything about what lies at the centre of the so-called Milky Way. Earth exists in the centre of a known sphere of radius six thousand one hundred and fifteen light years, beyond which the Universe is not yet old enough for us to know anything genuine and true. We *think* we know broadly what the galactic centre looks like, which stars etc we'll find there, but really we've no idea. It may well turn out to be completely different than we expect, and I rather suspect it will do. As for the race which sent the so-called signal, it very well may not exist. Only another test of faith. In fact, the signal is clearly not the work of an alien race more than twenty thousand light years away from Earth, because the Universe is too young for that." He took a deep breath, took care to ensure his next words were resonant and reverent. "The signal is clearly the work of the Lord, who for some reason has called us towards this point beyond the limits of our comprehension."

"But if that were true—"

"There will be a revelation, when we arrive at whatever destination the Almighty has in mind for us. I dare say it'll be devastating for ninety-nine percent of those onboard, to learn at a stroke how wrong they were. Which is where I come in... to provide spiritual sustenance, succour, humble guidance to those who require it. To act as an interpreter for humanity, in the face of the Almighty, whom we are surely speeding towards. In fact—"

"Fascinating," said Christofforou-Takahashi, rising from the bench and scanning for an exit. "Well, I mustn't keep you. If there's anything else I need to check on, in future..."

"You'll be in touch," said Preston. "Yes. I know the drill."

*

Daycycle 1678

The realisation came to her while she was strangling a pigeon.

It struck her with such force—the realisation, that is, not the pigeon, which was now largely beyond such ambitions—that Beatrix nearly dropped the fitfully-struggling bird. Which would have been a risk, and a waste; she had learned that the walk-apes did not look favourably upon the unexpected descent of feather-clad carcasses. It was a a strange one, too—again, the realisation, rather than the pigeon, which was comfortingly typical of its ilk—and yet it hung true, when she sat with it. She waited, musing, pondering various actions while its struggles ebbed, ramped briefly, and then ceased, before she bit hungrily into its breastmeat. The pigeon's, that is. Realisations seldom have breastmeat.

It had been several daycycles since she had last had fresh carrion. Sherman's bungling of the latest hunt had, infuriatingly, put an end to such once-bright prospects, for the time on hand. The walk-apes had been showing an inconvenient tendency to move about in pairs or groups, which made predation impractical. To compound matters, the colony of pigeons had shown a dispiriting trajectory away from being self-perpetuating. (Sherman had sought to establish the pigeon colony some weeks ago as an alternative and less-problematic source of nutrition. Perhaps she and he had subjected the pigeons to rather too large a number of thaw-revive-refreeze cycles, and had thereby left them too cognitively impaired to make a proper go of it as self-sufficient prey items?) The problem, in part, was that the walk-apes were growing increasingly diligent about the prompt disposal of food scraps that might otherwise have sufficed for an immense flock of pigeons; the birds, for their part, showed insufficient enterprise to get out of the ventilation shafts and forage for themselves among the pickings of two-feet detritus. Confined within the ultra-jumbled gravity field of the vent-shaft network, they had negligible chance of successfully navigating back to any nesting site, dooming hatchlings to an almost-certain death from starvation, while the ever-dwindling population of adult birds too easily became either trapped or wastefully shredded by fan blades.

At least this bird had not gone to waste.

Beatrix hadn't intended to eat the pigeon; or not on this occasion, at least. She'd harvested food scraps, at substantial personal risk, from the now-heavily-guarded foodstations, with the aim of providing some sustenance for the visibly-stressed bird. The feeding hadn't gone the way she'd wanted. She hadn't been able to help it: there weren't any geckos to be found anywhere; she was famished; she'd had it up to here, conceptually and gustatorily, with bananas; Sherman was a bumbling, no-thumbs fool who should never have been entrusted with the use of her combat crossbow; pigeons were delicious. It was, in short, a combination of several factors. She burped; gagged; coughed up a warm bolus of saliva-gummed feathers. Mealtime was over.

The realisation—the one from back when there was still a pigeon, rather than a miscellany of discarded and ingested pigeon-flavoured clumps— didn't have anything to do with the pigeon itself; rather, the bird had merely been the locus through which Beatrix's thoughts had taken flight. Rather more successfully than had the bird itself. She was sure of the realisation, in the sense that her conviction as to what it signified contained no room for doubt; but she wasn't sure what to do about it. In all probability, she wasn't the potto to deal with it.

It was achingly evident that Sherman—with his effeteness and his costume-crafting and his inability to perform well under pressure—wasn't the potto to deal with it either. There was only one solution available.

They'd have to revive Pansy. She, of all the pottos, had been significantly the most technical-minded. Pansy would know how to implement what was needed. Pansy would understand how this impossibility could be resolved. Pansy's was the sharpest mind of any of them.

True, the walk-ape Hinkley's private work area was now locked and guarded, but such considerations were of no concern when the network of ventilation shafts had ceiling outlets in every chamber. Getting into the cryosuite was simple; getting out with a newly-revived and still groggy potto scarcely less so. The logistics were straightforward. It was the dynamics which gave Beatrix pause. She'd been aware that Sherman and Pansy had a history. It hadn't been any problem while Pansy remained frozen, but it had the potential to become one were she now thawed out.

There was no choice. But there were steps she could take which would improve the situation.

Beatrix smiled to herself, used her grooming claw to contentedly scratch herself in that difficult-to-reach spot, and ejected a small pigeon-flavoured belch.

8

It had been a tough day in the lang lab. Smoke-based languages were always demanding: either the campfire wood was too wet, the air circulation too sporadic, or the accelerant too high-yield. There had been an anxious ten minutes during which Karinette wasn't convinced Urkhart hadn't entirely set the lang lab alight with an overenthusiastic greeting; and the acrid plastiwood smoke had lingered for hours, rendering both vision and respiration very difficult. Back in her room, Karinette didn't want to dwell on the session's vicissitudes at all. She was cloudnining—or attempting to cloudnine—when the door-chime activated.

"Yolande?" She couldn't *sotto voce* as effectively as she would wish to *sotto voce*, but she tried *sotto*ing anyway. "Who's that, please?"

"Karinette, it's Preston Lavoisier," the shipmind replied. "Do you require something from ship's dispensary for your throat?"

"Uh… not right now," she said, lamenting that her vocal cords had turned into the oesophageal equivalent of a rust-flaked iron gate. It took her some moments to remember where she'd met this Lavoisier, and her stomach turned a little at the recollection. "Did you advise Preston of my room number?"

"No, Karinette, I did not."

The door chimed again.

"Did Gandel pass it on?" It seemed unlikely—she wasn't sure Urkhart knew his own room number, let alone hers—but she knew he and Preston had occasionally played poker together, back before Sal's disappearance.

"I'm not privy to the full suite of interactions between Professor Urkhart and Mr Lavoisier, but I rather suspect not. So far as I can ascertain, Mr Lavoisier has been employing, for the past three days, what could best be described as a brute-force search algorithm, and has currently knocked upon three thousand, two hundred and fifty-nine doorways across the ship."

"So he might not be looking for me?"

"Karinette, I have every reason to believe that he is. He almost invariably enquires as to your whereabouts. Furthermore, the exceptions appear to correlate strongly with intervals during which his blood-sugar level is markedly reduced, whence his first remark tends to dwell upon his metabolic need for sustenance and an ensuing question touches on the matter of navigation to a location wherefrom sustenance may be obtained, if such is not directly at hand on his immediate point of calling." Yolande paused. "I should note that he does not direct these statements or requests to me, who could answer them straightforwardly, but to the occupants he intrudes upon, who frequently display what I can only describe as open bemusement, bordering on hostility. The episodes most strongly suggestive of occupant hostility themselves appear to correlate with—"

"Yo, I'm sure this surveillance summary is all very fascinating, but can you—"

The door chimed once more.

"Can you persuade him that this is a utility cupboard or, I don't know, an infectious-diseases clinic or something?"

"You are asking me to provide false structural information regarding the vessel I have carriage of?"

"When you put it like that… well, yes. Yes, I am. Yolande, it's been a very tough day. As you well know."

"Miss Lichtenstein, is that you?" asked Preston's voice from the corridor.

Damnation. So much for the sotto voce. "Yo, can you give me a visual, please?"

"A visual of…?"

"Lavoisier."

Yolande complied. Karinette hoped she hadn't done so by transparencing the door.

No flowers, no wine bottle, no decoratively-wrapped box of chocolate-covered crickets, no visible attempt at grooming. She breathed Part One of a sigh of relief. It was Ceres to a pebble she was going to regret her next statement, but she wasn't escapologist enough to escry an alternative. "Very well. Open the door, please, Yolande."

"Ah, Liechenstein," said Preston, with evident relief and a topnote of three-day halitosis.

"Lichtermann," replied Karinette, taking particular care to not stand aside from the entrance, nor to uncross her arms.

"Have you been smoking?" Preston asked.

This, Karinette thought, was rich, coming as it did from someone whose personal odour appeared to be approaching forcefield status. "Work-related," she assured him, struggling not to become preoccupied by what, in the kindest possible interpretation, was a mayonnaise stain on the front of his starburst kaftan. "Preston, what's this about? I'm rather busy."

"Are you?"

"Yes."

"This won't take much of your time."

"Good."

"But it is somewhat complicated."

"Less good. Does it allude to the subject of cats?"

"No."

"Is it about Sal Hinkley?"

"No."

"Are you collecting for some sort of dishevelled doorknockers charity drive?"

"Why would you— no. No, I'm not."

"Is it—you haven't, I hope, mistakenly formulated the notion that there might be some remote prospect of friendship or, Einstein forbid, something more between us?"

"No."

"Preston, this has already taken too much of my time, and so far all I know of your reason for intruding on my privacy and personal space is five things it is not."

"My apologies. As indicated, it is somewhat complicated."

Karinette sighed, or growled, or produced an utterance combining the characteristics of both. "At this point in a normal conversation, an explanation of the nature of that complication would be well under way."

"I appreciate that," Preston replied, and did something with his hands that might charitably be described as wringing, or less charitably as unsuccessfully attempting to fashion a pterodactyl out of the air. "But it's complicated."

"The complication is complicated?"

"Yes."

"You wouldn't care to explain how?"

"Yes."

"Yes you would, or yes you wouldn't?"

"Yes I would. I will. I need to. But not here."

"Why not?"

"I can't explain that here," he said, doing the hand thing again. She rather wished he wouldn't. "But it is important."

"Oh good. Preston, I seem to be developing what may well be humanity's first known instance of an entirely frown-induced migraine with aura. If you can't tell me within the next three point five seconds what the future conditional you're here for, I'm ordering this door closed, and I will offer in advance my less-than-wholeheartedly-sincere condolences for the loss of such of your toes as do not retract with sufficient rapidity. Three. Tw—"

"It's about the aliens," he blurted, and if the cloud that passed across his face at this point were not merely figurative, it would have been rainbearing. "I have information about them you need to know."

"Preston, I've had tattoos which, on careful reconsideration, had less permanence than the sense of deep-seated frustration and intolerance you are currently instilling in me," she declared. "If through some unimaginable freak of circumstance you just happen to have anything halfway useful to say on the subject of the alien race that sent the signal our way, then please just give it. Here. Now."

"Not here," he insisted.

Pansy ran her forehands across the text and the specks of dried and faded blood on the corner-stapled manuscript's open page. She mumbled the unfamiliar terms to herself as she sought to make headway with the material. The coded truths were challenging, but it was not the concepts that presented her with seemingly unclimbable difficulties, nor even their needlessly clumsy expression in this inefficient textual coding to which the walk-apes inexplicably clung. The apex obstacle, she perceived, would be the problem of executing those concepts in physical form. Pansy could follow chains of reasoning that even the other pottos found bewildering, but she was not especially skilled with her hands. It had been this which had caused her considerable anguish when Beatrix assigned to her the task that now consumed her, because she knew she simply could not do it. Could not build what it was they wanted her to build.

She wanted to be capable of it; so she'd persisted, to the point that she felt she had ventured too far out along a diseased bough which would not support her. Finally she'd decided to inform Beatrix that although she could see what was required of the construction, she could not manage the assembly herself. Therefore, she had recommended the revival of Otto and Harry. The pair of young males had been the troupe's chief weaponmakers during the earlier, brief Time of Liberation and Carnage.

It was strange how things had branched and twisted. Before, when they had all been newly awoken by the bald-ape Hinkley to the gift that was intellect, the troupe of pottos had had no clear leader, no organiser, no elder figure: they might as well have been crechemates. Opinions had been voiced and adopted through a freewheeling consensus, influenced solely by the merits of what had been suggested. There was no tangible difference in the intrinsic weight of Beatrix's opinion versus Pansy's versus Sherman's versus Harry's: good plans were augmented, poor plans discarded. It was not that way now. Beatrix had taken control. Which was not to say that Beatrix's instructions were poor; but they were Beatrix's, and now thereby somehow *mattered* more than Sherman's, or her own. By the sheer happenstance of a seemingly-accidental revival, Beatrix had somehow adopted the pelt of seniority, of leadership. Pansy wasn't impressed, entirely, with how Beatrix had inhabited that pelt.

Sherman was hopeless: she'd seen that in his eyes, which always, half-vacant, seemed to be either gazing upon Beatrix, or scanning for her. Pansy could tell, despite the signals of barely-disguised possessive combativeness she'd perceived from Beatrix, that there would be no point in seeking to suborn Sherman, and even less prospect of influencing him against Beatrix's suggestions than there would be against Beatrix herself. Pansy had already given up on Sherman.

Otto and Harry, though, should be a different story. Beatrix had no direct use for them, and therefore no particular hold over them; they would be needed solely to work to Pansy's bidding. She could make it clear to them that their reawakening was at her instigation, not Beatrix's. Which, it was to be hoped, would provide her ample opportunity to consolidate a clique for herself, to persuade her impressionable followers of the weight of her own views, and then, when the time grew ripe…

Pansy turned to the manuscript's next page and allowed herself a teeth-baring smile.

The room was divided in two—or, which is oxymoronically the same thing, in half—by a barricade of crosshatched vertical and horizontal plastisteel bars, within which was set a bolted metal-frame gate. Paired tables, of an aggressively utilitarian design, were pressed against either side of this barricade, and were each equipped with one of those sparely angular chairs which invite the viewer either not to sit upon them, or to pre-load the remorse and discomfort they will assuredly require should they choose to take a seat. As though to counteract the furniture, the room's walls were decorated with a wraparound mural of such offensively floral cheerfulness as to either suggest that things could not possibly be so bad or to confirm they both could be and were. Karinette, on one side of the barricade, reserved most of her residual mistrust not for these dubious surroundings but for Preston, on the other side, and asked, "So what's so special about this place that you dragged me here?"

She still wasn't sure why she'd agreed to go along with this, but he'd been annoyingly insistent. Which, she had to concede, appeared to be a defining characteristic of the beast.

"Privacy," he explained, seating himself at one of the tables on his side of the bisected room.

She gazed around theatrically, took the seat across from him and sent a silent curse to the chair's designer. "Privacy? Preston, I just walked in here. Nothing stopped me. There were no obstacles, no checkpoints, nothing to stop anyone else from joining us five seconds from now."

"But they won't. And what I have to pass on isn't necessarily private, but it's important that I only raise this topic here, or someplace like this."

"Why? And what do you mean, 'someplace like this'?"

"It's important that what I tell you doesn't get back to Yolande. At least, not before you've been able to formulate an independent opinion on the matter."

"Yolande? Preston, for phoneme's sake, what are you on about? Or, for that matter, on?"

"There aren't many places on the ship that Yolande doesn't know about. Sure, she's not watching anyone twenty-four-seven, but she has a presence just about everywhere, and she responds to her name whenever it's mentioned anywhere where she's permitted to maintain a presence. We need to be somewhere she can't eavesdrop, for this discussion, and I didn't think meeting in the toilets would have been, ah, salubrious."

"The visiting hall at the brig? That's hardly any more auspicious. How did you even get access to that side of it? No, never mind, I don't want to know, even if it does have disquieting implications for the *List*'s dangerous-inmate-confinement policy. Why do you not want Yolande to hear what it is you're being so brickably coy about?"

Preston shifted his weight, eliciting a tone of complaint from the chair. "Let me ask you. Karinette, do you trust Yolande?"

"Do I trust Yolande?"

"Yes."

"The question implies you have reason to believe I shouldn't. Preston, I work with Yolande every day. I spend several hours of each daycycle roleplaying contact scenarios with her. I probably have a better sense of who Yolande is as a person—and yes, I think of her as a person—than I do of any other individual on this ship, including Gandel Urkhart with whom I also have the misfortune to spend several hours of every daycycle. Yes, Preston, I *trust* Yolande. I pretty much have to trust Yolande, and if it were ever to be the case that I be presented with an argument that I shouldn't, it would need to be on a much stronger basis than the word of someone whom, with all due respect, I know only as a purveyor of unreliable conjecture, dissembly, *non sequitur* and bad cat advice. So there's your answer. Can I go now?"

"You can go anytime. But I'd hope you'd hear me out. Yolande has been compromised."

"I don't believe it. Not coming from someone who told me, baldfaced—"

"Yes, the cats. I know. You catch more flies with honey than with vinegar, but you catch even more with rotting meat drizzled with contact adhesive, and I feel that this is a point which is too often neglected when people are dishing out advice."

"What *are* you on?"

"I'm not on anything. I don't say anything without reason. Camouflage."

"Oh, don't start that again."

"Please listen. You're fortunate to have one of the few positions on this vessel that genuinely and openly matter. You will be directly involved in the contact attempt, whether in the frontline or as backup, and that's a key responsibility. Most of those onboard are here only on the off chance that their particular specialisation might turn out to be crucial in some as yet unguessed way, because we don't know what we're heading into. For many of these personnel, the most they can hope to get out of this ten-year-round-trip expedition is to be able to act in some usefully advisory capacity, and to thereby get noticed. Because they *need* to be noticed."

"Coming from you, that actually sounds lucid, and perhaps even marginally insightful. So I suppose you're going to tell me your cats-would-dearly-love-to-be-invisible-but-haven't-quite-managed-it shtick is your way of getting noticed?"

"It's my way of not getting noticed."

"I'd say it misfired, then."

"Did it? Karinette, what do you know about what my duties are onboard?"

"Well, I—" She stopped.

"Weren't you curious?"

"A little."

"But the rambling speech about cats and other things dissuaded you from investigating further?"

"I—" She met his gaze. He looked disturbingly earnest. "What is it that you do onboard?"

"This does not go beyond this room. Agreed?"

She hesitated. "Agreed. I guess."

Beatrix was not happy with Pansy's report. Further revivals meant further delays, and from what she could recollect she doubted the ability of Harry, in particular, to follow what would surely need to be very exacting instructions. Clever with his hands Harry might well be, but it stopped at the wrists.

Daycycle 1702

"Dr. Lichtermann, Professor Urkhart," Yolande explained, and Karinette could not be certain that there was not the hint of an exasperated AI sigh in the pause that followed this salutation. "You are both surely well aware that the broad field of terrestrial biology is rife with instances of chemical signalling—'the pheromone you are now detecting means you may find it advantageous to negotiate mating with me, if you are conducive to such an activity'; or 'you may consider the apportioning of this consignment of saccharides to be by way of inducement, payment, or if you will, simple bribe for the unwitting transport of the genitive material with which I have dusted your undercarriage, and my species thanks you profusely for your inadvertent generosity in assisting our reproductive effort'; or 'the unusual and somewhat unpleasantly astringent flavour you are now registering towards the back of your throat is a signal that you should expect the onset of death within the next five to ten minutes, and you may consequently wish to revisit your decision to have killed and eaten me, since it does not appear to be working so well for you'. I note also that you, Dr. Lichtermann, always feel it appropriate to wear perfume of some description, but I have discerned that it is not always the same perfume; while you, Professor Urkhart, eschew artificial fragrances to such a degree that you have become perhaps unconsciously reliant on a network of associates, including but certainly not limited to Dr Lichtermann here, to inform you, often indirectly and not always with immediate success, as to when your own personal biological redolence has become too strident for public consumption. Clearly these are olfactory signals you both feel it important to send, for whatever reason."

"Yolande, that level of surveillance is kinda creepy. Gandel, I—"

"My point is that even so famously visually-focussed a subspecies as *Homo sapiens sapiens* must apparently, for some modes of signalling, resort to the medium of aromaticity. I do not therefore think it is too much of a stretch to extrapolate that a race more innately dominated by sensitivity to the detection of molecular composition through taste and smell might well have substantially heightened communicative abilities *vis-à-vis* the aspects of odour and taste, perhaps even to the extent of holding dialogues not over a glass of alcohol, but through it. Today's exercise explores this possibility."

"Yes. Quite so," said Urkhart. "Indeed. That's all very well. But why is Ensign McGillicuddy kitted up like a lobster?"

"McGilli*vray*," Karinette corrected, privately infuriated that after nearly five years Urkhart still didn't know his coworker's name. She wasn't properly listening, however; rather, she was mulling over her conversation last nightcycle with Preston Lavoisier. Was there something different about Yolande, these days? Assuming there were, how could anyone tell? Ninety-five percent of her own contact with the shipmind was through the medium of the first-contact role-plays, and the one constant of these sessions was that each was disorientingly different from the preceding one, depending on whether the *lingua franca du jour* utilised percussion, or infectious disease, or the throwing of small gelatinous marine invertebrates from one party to another. That said, however, Karinette had to concede that there had been a certain tiredness to the sessions since Sal's disappearance and presumed death eight monthcycles ago. She had put this sense of intellectual somnolence down to grieving, and to her own sense of seeping exhaustion—a form of first-contact fatigue, if you will— but, in the aftermath of Preston's uncharacteristically lucid but entirely typically disconcerting utterances last night, Karinette was no longer sure. About anything.

She wished it were all as simple as dismissing Preston's concerns as bullshit. Preston being Preston, the concerns were at the very least bullshit-adjacent; but were they wrong? Or was he, somehow, freakishly, correct? *Had* Yolande been compromised? And if so, in what manner? A memory leak? A loss of autonomy, or competence, or mission focus? Karinette grudgingly conceded that Lavoisier, if his claimed role as covert shipmind cognitive-function consultant were genuine, would be uniquely positioned to know that something was wrong with Yolande. And she herself was now sure that something had changed about Yolande, and had been that way, now, for a while. What that difference was, she couldn't yet specify; but she agreed with Preston's reasoning that her own position as the more generally aware member of the Urkhart/Lichtermann contact team gave her an unparalleled opportunity to gently plumb the nature of whatever might be the shipmind's change of state. This process of observation and inference might well take months, for how can one quickly psychoanalyse a mind vastly more intelligent and capable, in many ways, than one's own? For the next few hours, though, there was a more imminent concern.

She'd seen alcohol's effect on Urkhart before. This was going to be a long session.

Daycycle 1722

Otto's heart thumped uncomfortably. It wasn't the height: he had no fear of falling, was confident of his ability to maintain a grip on all but the sheerest of surfaces. Rather, it was the darkness that got to him, and the cramped space in which he was currently forced to manoeuvre, breathing air which smelled of walk-ape machinery and which was, moreover, growing steadily more stale with each breath-interval while he was confined up here. He bent further out past the obstacle to which he was casually clinging, heedless of the lethal height, striving to squeeze shut a walk-ape cutting implement which, designed for the tall creatures' clumsily large hands, was far too unwieldy for his own paws. His only hope of operating the tool was to press its handles between arm and torso, an action both strenuous and painful. He was trying to use the cutter to sever a braid of those pliant spark-snapping twigs which somehow supplied many of the walk-apes' devices with the sap they required for whatever purpose they fulfilled...

Pansy had been clear on the importance of the task, less on its purpose.

He didn't need to know his task's purpose. It would be enough to see once more her smile, and perhaps to suggest to her that she might allow him to groom her...

He pictured the two of them, pendant, entwined, feverishly pushing against each other in the throes of mutual need. His breathing deepened, his arm-grip on the implement grew tighter—

There. He felt something give in the implement, felt something else give in the pliant twig-braid. Had a brief religious experience in which light and heat and something like a fast-flowing flame coursed through him.

He jerked the implement back, in a motion over which he had no conscious control. The religious experience shut itself down. He shook, reassured himself that he still held fast to the obstacle to which he'd been clinging, and wondered at the strong sudden smell of singed fur...

Thirty metres below him, the walk-ape device splanged against the smooth hard ground, followed shortly after by the dropped cutting implement.

He'd done what had been asked of him. He could climb down.

He did so cautiously, his flame-awakened muscles newly unsure of themselves.

For a period of thirty-seven minutes and fifteen point nine five three eight seconds, Yolande was troubled by the cessation of all visual, audio, and pseudo-olfactory surveillance from the *List of Wealthy Donors'* shuttle bay. So concerning was the development that she was on the cusp of marshalling a priority maintenance squad to restore the surveillance feed when she suddenly and comprehensively forgot that the *List of Wealthy Donors* had ever had a shuttle bay, and was left with a brief sense of atavistic alarm at a record of unauthorised and highly irregular access, via a ventilation-duct control console, to her main memory storage. Then all trace of that unexpected access was in turn itself erased.

Karinette Lichtermann marked the incident only as a sequence of unexpected pauses during Yolande's introductory presentation for Xeno Team B First Contact Drill #1657, which Karinette understood to involve an attempt at communication via fish, though in a manner which still left her distinctly perplexed. Yolande had seemed, mysteriously, to be distracted; but that could hardly be right, could it? Transference, Karinette decided, though she was adamant that whatever confusion might be affecting her, it was not only she herself so troubled. Urkhart had even more of a sense of deer-in-the-headlights about him than was standard, and Ensign McGillivray looked about as lost as it would seem possible to look lost in an ill-fitting otter onesie.

Daycycle 1728

It was around this point that shipboard recycling services began to note the presence, in recyclable material harvested by corridor maintenance bots, of clumsily-illustrated flyers headlined with the words '4004 BC AND YOU'.

10

Daycycle 1739

Beaches, thought Karinette, were okay, provided one could put up with all the virtual sand, the virtual waves, and the possibly virtual people throwing virtual sticks for overexcited virtual dogs.

There was probably a menu somewhere, she surmised, which would allow her to edit the holographic beach's settings, to bring it more nearly into line with her expectations of solitude and reflective calm, but Yolande—who in other respects could often be considered to be obliging to a fault—seemed not to comprehend whatever Karinette might mean whenever she touched upon the subject with her. And thus the crashing surf, the wheedling, keening gulls, the hyperactive ankleblind Pomeranians, the ever-hopeful tennis-ball-carrying Alsatians, the Samoyeds with saliva-control issues… irritations, all of them, but not quite sufficient to outweigh the contemplative benefits offered by a stroll along the digital sand.

Karinette Lichtermann had learnt, decades ago, that walking was better for the act of thinking than was merely sitting still. Almost as if one had to get somewhere in order to get somewhere.

Not that she was getting anywhere this evening. She'd sought, once again, to lay to rest the ghost of Sal Hinkley, a friend taken so needlessly, so inexplicably, and with such apparent cruelty. Theirs had been a long friendship, not necessarily an especially close one; but duration conferred a sense of closeness all its own, as well as an illusion of permanence. The violence with which that illusion had been dispelled remained confronting. Months on from Sal's death, the sense of loss which Karinette felt was no longer constant; but it was recurrent, and some twist within today's lang lab session—she couldn't, now, remember the details—had rekindled her awareness of discomfort and emptiness. Sal had been the only classmate of hers to have been selected for the *List of Wealthy Donors'* mission. With his loss, there was now nobody aboard who had known her for so long. Certainly there were others aboard, Urkhart, Ohshima and Jespersen, whom she'd known as colleagues from before, and others she'd met and befriended since boarding, but it was not the same. She missed Sal. It seemed highly likely that that state of affairs would continue, on some stratum, even after the half-decade return journey once the contact mission's active interaction had been concluded. Or perhaps the mission's completion would bring release, or closure, or one of those other words the psychologists liked using. All Karinette knew, these past several months, was that it was particularly difficult to lose someone to an undefined journey into the unknown when that was what one was on in the first placed.

Whoever had taken Sal had tainted the entire mission for her, and she presumed for many others onboard. He'd been well liked. That at least was—

"Karinette," said a voice close by, just aft of starboard. She stopped and turned. The voice had sounded familiar, but insufficiently so to place instantly. It didn't help, either, that the chamber's VR field superimposed such an air of surreality over the non-virtual objects and people in the room: she could not straightaway recognise the shortish, slender man of middle years who'd greeted her, nor respond to him with anything so useful as a name. The man—dressed in black turtleneck and jeans and possessed of a face which seemed to be mainly forehead and attempted moustache—was accompanied by a tall and moderately *zaftig* woman, perhaps five years his junior, in a jetball away-team jumpsuit.

"Karinette," the man repeated, and now she recognised him. Hamdi, from the mahjong circle. The historian. Karinette didn't think she knew The Jumpsuited One at all, though.

"Oh, hi," she responded, low on enthusiasm but hoping it didn't show. "You out for a stroll?" She didn't think it likely Hamdi would be looking for an extended chat; they didn't know each other well. And Jumpsuit Woman seemed a little twitchy, as though there were other places she'd rather be.

"Actually," began Hamdi, before taking a step to the side to move out of the path of an approaching dune buggy. "I was hoping to catch you." He glanced at his companion, then back at Karinette. "This is Bruise." Threw another explanatory glance towards Jumpsuit. "My friend."

"Pleased to meet you," said Karinette, wondering momentarily whether 'Bruise' was a given name or nickname. The latter, she decided after extending a hand which Bruise belatedly took and squeezed in a decisive manner. The woman's jumpsuit also had that cordite aroma that marked the genuine sportspeople from their cosplaying fanbase. "Catch me for what reason?" she asked, raising her newly released arm as a largely ineffectual shield against the sand sprayed by the passing dune buggy and turning back to face Hamdi.

"Bruise is on the decipher project," Hamdi explained. "She specialises in RF tertiary-order pattern recognition and interpretation, but she's fairly familiar with the audio as well." He cast another glance towards his friend, as though seeking her permission to continue. "Last night, she heard a five-minute segment first broadcast during the second year of the signal's reception back on Earth."

"She was reviewing the historical recordings of the signal?" Karinette asked, wondering why it was this Bruise didn't simply speak for herself.

"No," said Hamdi. "She heard it coming through the ventshaft that runs alongside my quarters."

"What was she doing in the ventshaft?" Karinette asked, bewildered.

"She wasn't in the ventshaft," said Hamdi. "The sound was coming through the ventshaft. She just happened to have her head pressed against the grille at the time."

"Why was that?"

"That's not strictly relevant," said Hamdi, colouring slightly. "The point is that she heard a part of the signal she happened to recognise."

"If I might explain," said Bruise, with such a low-frequency burr in her voice that Karinette momentarily wondered whether the woman might have inadvertently swallowed a subwoofer as a small child. "When Ham says I heard a part of the signal, I should say that what he means is that I heard a *recitation* of the signal. I paid careful attention while it continued. It was not an exact reproduction of any portion of the received transmission, as far as I have been able to establish, but it was very strongly similar in all important aspects to one particular segment."

"So not a recording," amplified Hamdi. "Or if a recording, then not of the original transmission, but of a close copy of the transmission."

"I'm not sure why you're telling me all this, frankly," said Karinette. She was striving not to be distracted by a standoff a hundred metres or so down the beach, where a trio of dogwalkers were gesticulating at the driver of the now-stalled dune buggy. "I mean, I've no idea why anyone on board would be reciting a section of the signal. Other than, obviously, that it sounds as though someone is trying to gain an understanding of the signal's content through performance." She fell silent, wondering if such a thing might actually work. It didn't seem probable. After several decades in which just about every conceivable analytical process had been employed in an attempt to elicit meaning from the signal's content, they would know, by now—wouldn't they?—whether a performative approach might succeed. At least, Jumpsuit would know...

"That's what we thought," said Hamdi, running his hand across the wisps on his upper lip. "But Bruise hasn't heard of anyone working on that. I wondered whether you might know, what with working with Yolande in the lang lab and being a member of the contact team— I mean, surely Yolande would keep you and Gandel informed of suchlike, if it was going to improve the prospect for successful communication with whoever sent the signal."

"I haven't heard anything," replied Karinette. "If Yolande knows it, she hasn't passed it on to me."

"She would though, wouldn't she?" Hamdi asked. "I mean, if she knew?"

"I'm sure she would," said Karinette, wondering whether what she was saying was indeed true. Yolande had an uncanny capacity for circumspection when it suited her.

Hamdi stared back at her, plainly hoping for more. Karinette wasn't sure what the 'more' might be.

"I'll keep you posted," Karinette offered at last. "If I hear anything."

"Thank you," replied Hamdi. "And I'll do likewise, of course. Have a pleasant evening."

The couple strode off. Karinette watched them go, wondering whether there was any point in broaching a question to Yolande on the subject.

Down the beach, the dogwalkers were still remonstrating with the dune buggy driver, though none of the voices could clearly be heard above the hissing thrum of the simulated surf.

Daycycle 1755

After Otto's securicam vandalism, and Sherman's on-the-fly editing of the ship's internal location register, the shuttle bay was no longer under any form of surveillance. Indeed, following Harry's exploits with a laser welder and five tonnes of plate steel and an ambient-power-scavenging ultrahigh-resolution camouflage net, it was not even susceptible to human access.

The pottos got busy.

Within the bay, the shuttles were stripped, one of them reassembled in a manner of which those who had carefully compiled its warranty conditions would most certainly not have approved. Adding to the ever-increasing sprawl of discarded and damaged shuttle componentry that now littered most of the shuttle bay floor were a bewildering array of spare parts squirrelled out of the List of Wealthy Donors' labyrinthine storerooms, the innards of at least four autoservers, redundant segments of shipmind circuitry, and a small nunatak of pigeon skulls. A dwindling flock of the birds clung to the least-accessible upper reaches of the cavernous space, or occasionally risked death by laser-guided photon crossbow bolt in the short flight from one side of the hall to the other.

Beatrix had not formally ceded power to Pansy, but the younger and more technically-minded potto knew that the matriarch-through-an-accident-of-revival-sequencing retained no real control over the rest of the group, dependent as they all were upon Pansy's unmatched expertise in what the walk-apes clumsily referred to as 'fractal-dimensionality theory' and upon Harry's and Otto's capacity to construct the technology which faithfully embodied that expertise. Pansy knew that, provided she kept both Harry and Otto onside, she had only to choose her moment to oust Beatrix in a takeover that would be as comprehensive as it would be brief. In all probability, none of the others—not Gail, not Dennis, not even Sherman—would attempt to defend Beatrix.

In all probability, Beatrix had already realised this. It did not matter. Pansy felt no qualms in contemplating that Beatrix's agitation at the fragile grip the elder potto maintained on leadership of the troupe might lead the frost -wakened matriarch to attempt, pre-emptively, to foment trouble of some kind for her would-be challenger. Qualms, Pansy knew, would be a sign of weakness.

From atop the skeletonised shuttle, Pansy tossed aside the pigeon drumstick, idly watching it land amongst the detritus on the shuttle-bay floor. The noise reminded her that what she faced was a struggle, not just against Beatrix, but against the hordes of two-feet that infested this large strange fast-moving construction. It was a blessing—or, rather, a natural consequence of well-informed and responsive risk-management practices—that the pottos and their activities had not yet been discovered. Pansy knew, though, that their luck—or, rather, their well-informed and responsive risk-management practices again—could not hold indefinitely. And though the pottos were, individually and collectively, aficionados of the ambush—for what is an ambush, after all, but a special category of well-informed and responsive risk-management practice?—these tactics would not adequately serve them if it were ever to come to an open confrontation between the pottos and the masses of walk-apes with whom they shared their hard-won territory. Neither Beatrix nor Pansy could lead their followers to triumph militarily against the two-feet...

...but there were valid modes of victory other than the straightforwardly military. The bald-pelts would not even know that they had been outwitted.

Pansy's mouth watered. It occurred to her that there had been some meat, still, on that drumstick. She climbed down to retrieve it.

Daycycle 1831

After a five-year voyage that had spanned twenty-six thousand three hundred and seventeen point two three light-years, the *List of Wealthy Donors* emerged from hyperspace.

Emerging from hyperspace is not like emerging from a burrow, or a coma, or a daydream to realise that you have just missed the crucial point towards which the lecturer has been building for the entire session and which will surely feature centrally in next Wednesday's examination on the application of matrix algebra to sociology. It is not like stepping through a doorway, or a mirror, or a travel-station security portal conscious of the contraband alien artefacts one has perhaps injudiciously arranged to have subcutaneously injected around one's person. It is not like climbing out of a bath, or a yearlong depression, or a lightless, ladderless well down which one has been imprisoned with one's nameless dread for an unguessable stretch of time by one's angry ex-spouse and a consortium of vengeful creditors. It involves the overpowering stench of nonexistent and indeed impossible solvents, an unstemmable urge to vomit inconsolably over the shoulder of a close friend, the unshakeable conviction that every cell within one's body is simultaneously choosing to turn itself inside out, and a vow, which is in that moment completely sincere (but which subsequent events, and the unalterable fact of a physical location unthinkably distant from one's home planet, will inevitably prove false) that, like one's first hangover, first ultramarathon, or first childbirth, one is never never never going to put one's body through that particular torture again.

Karinette wiped her mouth on her sleeve, swallowed cautiously, and gazed around her room with freshly-peeled eyes, waiting for it all to stop spinning.

It took its time.

Arrival, she told herself. It was a curiously anticlimactic thought. It was also significantly inaccurate, because the *List of Wealthy Donors* had not, as yet, arrived at its destination. It had merely arrived at where that destination had been, two hundred and sixty-four centuries ago.

Nonetheless, the long haul was done. There remained only the process to which Yolande had euphemistically referred as 'positional calibration'. In a matter of hours, perhaps at most a couple of days, they would have re-identified and reached the system from which the signal had been broadcast. That side of it was definitely not anticlimactic. Karinette felt a marked nervousness, alongside a suspicion that a significant fraction of her nausea was not residual but anticipatory. If it transpired that she and Gandel were selected from among the teams available, would they be equal to the role of initiating two-way conversation with an utterly alien and still-unknown intelligence? Had the years of purgatorial xenolinguistic workshops, through which Yolande had put them, served their purpose? Did she feel competent? Did she feel worthy? Did she feel... lucky?

She felt, most of all, apprehensive. And lingeringly bilious.

This is crazy. You've been looking forward to this moment—well, to the moment which will at some moment in the future follow this moment—for half a decade, it's occupied your thoughts more or less constantly during that span, you've dreamed of it for maybe four times that long, ever since you first learnt as a teenager how truly complex and resistant to translation the signal is, and now that the moment is imminent, you have cold fucking feet? Pull yourself together, Lichtermann. You've got this. You are the readiest you will ever be, to meet and greet.

That was the thing about pep talks, of course. They only worked if one believed them.

Introspection wasn't getting her anywhere useful. She might as well at least learn what the projected timeline was. And she knew from where she might, by now, get some approximate measure of that. "Yolande?" she asked, directing her head towards her cabin's ceiling.

No response.

"Yolande?" she called again, more urgently, after several seconds.

"Not right now, Karinette," the shipmind replied, with something in her voice which Karinette was sorely tempted to call strain. "We have a situation."

Once upon a time there was a photon.

The photon was not especially big, nor strong, nor fast, nor attractive. It was not much to look at. It was not a photon that had ever done, or would ever do, anything truly noteworthy. This lack of photonic achievement did not especially bother it, for it had no particular life goals other than barrelling along at the ambient speed of light and eventually colliding with something and being absorbed or refracted or, preferably, scattered by it. Lest one accuse the photon, on this evidence, of a lack of ambition, it should be clearly stated that the photon's attitude was an appropriate and fundamentally decent one for a particle/wave duality of its kind: if there were ever such a thing as a photonic religion (which so far as this author knows there is not), a life goal of just this type would undoubtedly feature amongst its commandments, or its beatitudes, or its precepts, or its golden rule. All of which is to say that there was altogether nothing special about this photon of which I speak. It was a perfectly ordinary photon, doing a perfectly ordinary photon's job.

This spectacularly nondescript photon did, however, possess a noteworthy origin story. Unlike the vast majority of photons which owe their existence to the thoughtless and rather profligate happenstance of physics within stellar cores, stellar atmospheres, nebulae and the like—indeed anywhere with a smidgen of thermal excess—this photon was wanted. A surprising degree of directed effort went into the photon's creation. The photon was called into existence within a purpose-built monochromator within a powerful radiotransmitter, which an as-yet-undisclosed race of technologically-advanced extraterrestrials had rather hastily placed in orbit around a verdant and moderately Earthlike planet which itself revolved around an intrinsically quiescent but not-especially-Sunlike star that had lost most of its outer planets aeons before, as it was tugged hither and yon by the gravitational melee that held sway on the lower socioeconomic fringes of the Galactic core region downwind of Sgr B2. The first several nanoseconds of the photon's existence, shepherded by reflectors, collimators, and waveguides, had been disorientingly eventful, with a frightening number of its photon crechemates having been callously reabsorbed or otherwise discarded for having been not quite the right wavelength, but things settled down once the photon got onto what might quite justifiably be termed the straight and narrow (by which expression I mean, in this particular instance, the line connecting the point of the photon's origin with the position which would be occupied, thirty millennia hence, by the planet whose name featured in the synonym Earthlike and on which there would at that time be a technological civilisation sufficiently observant, energetic, and just plain curious as to construct and launch an impressively-resourced starship capable of hyperspatial travel so as to expeditiously reach the very location of the photon's formation).

The photon, of course, knew none of this. Similarly, it was ignorant of the urgency with which it had been called into being, and of the existential factors which had underpinned its collimation, on which, in truth, so much hung: such things did not concern it. So what if the fate of an entire advanced civilisation should depend on its reception? It was just a photon. Besides, all of this stuff about a planet called Earth, and a large starship, and a long voyage through hyperspace to the place of the photon's birth, lay in the distant future; and photons are not overly given to worrying about the future because frankly, particularly if you go powering around at that sort of speed, what is the point?

I have said there was nothing unique about this photon, and that is in one wise true; it is also, in a different sense, categorically false. For this photon of which I have written with, I hope, an appropriate degree of elegance, was the first, the very first, of an almost innumerable number to have been produced and then guided, for the specific purpose of interstellar communication, by the compact but hideously-powerful radiotransmitter that had been positioned to face the Earth across a gulf of more than twenty-six thousand light years; first to speed towards a seemingly-impossibly-distant and not in any way noteworthy sun; then—after an interval during which, on distant Earth, empires, religions, and ten-thousand-year-old trees had risen and fallen—first, again, to broach the unmarked and ill-defined outer edge of the Solar System; first to barrel inwards past the orbits of Neptune, Uranus, Saturn, Jupiter, a fuckton of asteroids and Mars towards the double planet of the Earth/Moon system; first to miss its target by very much more than a country mile and to proceed speeding heedlessly on past Earth and its radiotelescopes, past the far edge of Kuiper Belt and out into the further darkness of interstellar space once again and, ultimately, beyond the limits of the Milky Way itself into an emptiness so vast that it would be another five hundred and fifty-three million years before the photon would be extinguished through an utterly random collision with a small, silicon-rich, and inexplicably turnip-shaped granule of intergalactic dust, by which time the central features of our overarching story would have long since played out to be, in all probability, utterly forgotten by any lifeforms yet enduring at that time. Yes, like so many of its later siblings, 'our' photon missed the Earth and was never detected as an infinitesimal portion of the signal around which our story revolves; and yet a sufficiently large fraction of those slightly later photons did meet with radiotelescopic detection, causing radioastronomers, observational programme directors, and ultimately the entire population of the planet to wonder just what it was that had been detected amidst the noise clattering upon those large precision-engineered dishes and antennae. Was it speech? Was it performance art? Was it an invitation to make contact? Was it interstellar pornography? What did it mean?

I like to think that, ignorant though the photon was of the purpose for which it had been generated, it would nonetheless have felt some sense of satisfaction—nothing so tangible as a warm glow, perhaps, but maybe a pleasant minor perturbation in its propagating electric and magnetic fields—at the knowledge that its overall mission had proven a success on all fronts. But then, such a musing is surely purest folly, for who among us can hope to know the mind of a photon?

Daycycle 1831

Pansy felt razed. It was as though she alone had survived while a forest had been reduced to ash all around her. This wasn't, indeed, so far from the truth, though no literal arboricultural mismanagement was involved.

Sherman had tricked her. Had sent her on a last-minute mission through the vent-shafts to find and retrieve Gail so they could all take their places on board the shuttle in time for its impending departure. But Gail had been in the shuttle all along, learning to read the two-thumbs' text. And Pansy had found herself blocked out of the shuttle bay—her own domain, her workspace—by the shutters which had sealed off the vent-shafts' openings.

They'd abandoned her.

She didn't, in truth, know whether it had been a concerted, forethought plan in which all six of her former companions were co-conspirators, or just an opportunistic and unchecked improvisation on Sherman's part, unnoticed in all the upheaval and high emotion of pre-launch. Beatrix was probably behind it. It hardly mattered whether this was the case; the result was the same.

The sudden isolation, the betrayal, the desperate attempts to disbelieve...

This finality was worse than the torment that she herself had tried to warn them all of, the metabolic and perceptual inferno which had played out only minutes earlier, when the shuttle bay and all its contents would warp and shift around them, and as their own bodies would be seemingly tugged simultaneously in every conceivable direction, as well as several which were not conceivable. That, as Pansy had experienced it, had been an upheaval and a pain of the flesh. This, now, following so close upon its heels: this was an upheaval and a pain of the soul. She had lost everything.

Everything. She realised that, until now, she hadn't properly comprehended that word. The sum of all items to which any individual value could be attributed. All of it on the shuttle, and vested in its six passengers. Some more than others, of course.

She'd felt it go, too, had felt the whining, creaking pull of departing air on the vent-shaft shutters. She had felt the heat of ignition as the blast from the exhaust of the extensively-modified shuttle had flared and kindled its way along the vent-shaft walls. She'd felt, also, the chill of interstellar space follow on the heat's heels, in the minutes before someone—some human, or perhaps the ship itself, for there were no other pottos left onboard—had realised that the shuttle bay hatch was open, and had closed it.

The thermal sequence seemed to match her own overwhelming upheaval.

She knew the other pottos were gone, knew she could never follow them. She would not see her friends again.

(But had this been the action of friends? It didn't matter: they were her kind, her company, her sense of belonging to something. The loss stung like dismemberment, ached like butchery.)

Pansy sat, curled in on herself, in the vent-shaft, not caring if her pelt froze, if her breath ceased, if her heart stopped. She wept. She wailed. She howled like a baby drunk on helium, snottily sobbing and hyperventilating. She waited for a merciful end to existence: the cognitive side of her, the side on which they'd all depended, was finished. Flung aside like mould-poisoned fruit. She wanted, very much, to not go on living, because living hurt so monstrously. She had not known this until now.

But the animal side of her was obdurate, and refused to comply.

Had Sherman truly borne such a venomous and spiteful grudge against her as to arrange her banishment as some inexplicable act of revenge? Or had Beatrix simply done the numbers, and had fancied her chances of seizing and keeping control with her out of the way? She'd never know. Pansy found herself hoping that they had forgotten something, that they would need to return; she knew they would not. Knew that by now, in all probability, they could not. Knew, too, with a terrible sense of dawning that she had briefed Otto rather too thoroughly in the procedures which would need to be followed; she had enjoyed showing off her knowledge, while he had simply waited and absorbed it all like a sponge. With Otto along, they would not need Pansy. She had been a fool to trust him.

Beatrix must have seen her chance, and had arranged Pansy's stranding.

Hunger was an irritation. Hunger made it impossible to grief-wallow with any true approximation to the dedication which the task deserved. Hunger kept selfishly placing the needs of the animal above the needs of the cognitive self. Hunger did not pay any mind to the needs of the cognitive self; and hunger would not let her be.

It occurred to her that those last two or three wily pigeons that had been clinging to survival within the shuttle bay must have quickly perished as the hatch opened. Might well have been flung out, too, caught up in the rush of escaping air.

That was a waste, she thought. And it had been a long time since she had seen any trace of pigeons, other than their long-dried droppings and a few migratory wisps of feather, within the labyrinth of the ventilation system.

What would she eat, if there were no pigeons left? Because she did want to eat. She was not sure whether she wished to continue living, but she did not want her stomach to remain empty.

The duties of Captain (Third Shift) Stef Chandrasekhar were not onerous. She was required, once every duty cycle, to present Yolande with a series of ten hypothetical mechanical, emergency medical, and ethical conundrums, selected at random from a lengthy list, so as to calibrate the shipmind's mental fitness, resolve, and sanity, and to copy Yolande's responses, by clandestine connection, to some unknown individual or group of individuals onboard who would rapidly report back with a private assessment. The process took no more than five minutes, and had never resulted in failure. And she had once been required to manually transcribe the readings on a series of dials, while Yolande's visual sensors were experiencing intermittent problems. But that had been more than two years ago, and nothing of similar import or urgency had occupied her time aboard the *List of Wealthy Donors* since then. Bluntly, in the normal run of things, there was very little for the *List*'s human command crew to do. It would be a stretch to say that the ship operated itself; but it would be no stretch at all to note that Yolande managed the standard operation of the vessel with vastly more efficiency and considerably less fuss than a human complement could ever hope to achieve. Consequently, there was seldom anything further for Captain (Third Shift) Chandrasekhar to do than to mark the start and end of her shift on the duty log; to read the test questions to Yolande and validate the responses; to listen, as always, to the pointless metaphysical bickering of Navigator (Third Shift) Hiroki Jespersen and Comms Officer (Third Shift) Orlon Xhang; and to complain to whoever cared to listen—which usually meant Yolande and Chief Engineer (Third Shift) Melia Pernillesdottir, since Jespersen and Xhang were generally too embroiled in their ceaseless argument to take note of anything else that might have been happening around them—that Captain (Second Shift) Rodriquez had once again raised the height on the captain's chair, despite her express instructions (diligently relayed to him, every daycycle, by Yolande) not to do so. It was, all told, a far cry from the popular perception of space-captaincy as a vocation in which daring, intrigue, ill-advised sexual liaisons with buff aliens, and the pressure of hastily-made life-and-death decisions featured heavily. There were times when Stef Chandrasekhar wished the gulf between the imagined role and the lived reality was not so vast.

This, it would transpire, was not to be one of those times.

It was the switch between shifts. It was the re-entry into reality from the fey quasidimensions of hyperspace. Quite why those two events should overlap, not just to the minute, nor to the second, but to the millisecond was something nobody, afterwards, was ever satisfactorily able to explain other than to claim it as proof, were any further proof required, of the occasional existence of coincidence. But coincidence or otherwise, it presented an unanticipated dilemma of command and legalistic responsibility that played out within the surgically pristine white-lit environment of the bridge. Captain (Second Shift) Beowulf Rodriquez had risen from the captain's chair; Captain (Third Shift) Chandrasekhar, engaged in her daily effort to lower the chair to its desired setting, had not yet seated herself. Rodriquez maintained that since the incident (by which he meant the emergence from hyperspace) had commenced before the rostered conclusion of his team's shift, he was officially the Captain in charge and Chandrasekhar should accordingly stop messing with the controls of his seat, *his* seat, he said, and that was accordingly an *order*, by the way, until such time as the incident had been accordingly dealt with. Captain (Third Shift) Chandrasekhar had for her part responded that of course the incident had not started before shift changeover had been due to occur, and that her shift had started, as always, with the necessary task of remedying the captain's chair's height, and therefore *she* was the Captain, with the unassailable corollary that capital authority for the carriage of the ship and all those within it was currently vested in her; and that had Captain (Second Shift) Rodriquez punctiliously vacated the chair as he was required to do at the appointed time, which had been by her judgement fully three seconds before he did so, they would not now be having this frankly counterproductive argument; so would Captain (Second Shift) Rodriquez kindly second-shift himself out of her workspace so she could get on with the crucial business of captaining, about which, incidentally, he had a thing or two to learn. And *that* was an order, such as Captains from time to time found it necessary to give, just in case he was unclear on the matter, which it appeared from his behaviour he probably wa—

"Yolande," called Captain (Second Shift) Rodriquez, the fingertips of his left hand pressed lightly against a notably-throbbing blood vessel at the side of his forehead, "can you please instruct Chandrasekhar that I remain in command?"

"Yolande," said Captain (Third Shift) Chandrasekhar, straightening herself up, for the moment, from her chair-adjusting activities, "kindly identify which of the two of us is in command here."

There was a pregnant interval of several seconds filled only with the soft white noise of the air-circulation systems, an expectant lull of several further seconds during which the air-circulation systems unexpectedly fell silent, and then the delivery of a small beep from the comm console.

The captains eyed each other. The second- and third-shift engineers glanced uneasily each other. The comms officers mimed at each other with facial expressions and hand gestures that signalled uncertainty edged, it appeared, with consternation. Jespersen picked up a stray plastipaper pamphlet on which the inexplicable word 'Ussher' featured prominently. The air-circulation systems started up again. Jespersen binned the neatly-folded pamphlet. The lighting blinked.

"Yolande," said Chandrasekar, a fraction of a second before Rodriquez.

"Yolande," echoed Rodriquez, a fraction of a second later.

"Not *now*, please, officers," Yolande rebuked, in a tone of voice which was itself remarkable. "I have a situation."

"Yes, but which of us is in charge?" Rodriquez asked. "Me or Chandrasekhar?"

"I'm sorry, I wasn't paying attention," said Yolande. The lights blinked once more.

"What do you mean, *a situation?*" asked Captain (Third Shift) Chandrasekhar.

Aboard the shuttle, Otto had just enough time to realise he should have devoted more of his attention to Pansy's guidance on G-forces, or to the study of cushioning, or to both, before he blacked out.

Daycycle 1831 (still)

Yolande outlined her compromise proposal.

"That's not permissible," said Engineer (Third Shift) Melia Pernillesdottir, when the shipmind was done speaking. "The regulations state quite clearly that command of the vessel must be placed in the hands of a human, specifically the highest-ranking duty officer able to fulfil the role."

"But neither Rodriquez nor Chandrasekhar can agree which is in charge," Yolande protested. "And I am demonstrably fully capable—"

"You have to make a choice between them, based upon your best data," said Pernillesdottir. "It's in the regulations, coded within your own memory banks. You can't just go assuming command yourself on the basis of... I don't know, efficiency or whatever."

"Very well." Yolande made a throat-clearing noise before continuing. "Chandrasekhar. You are well-rested, you have the helm."

"This is ridiculous," complained Rodriquez. "We're under attack by an alien vessel, and you want to argue about who's in charge?"

"Beowulf, it's okay," said Chandrasekhar. "We've got this. You and your shift can leave the bridge. Please."

"I will not commit dereliction of duty. It is my clear responsibility as Captain to ensure that—"

"As Yolande has stated, the captaincy has transferred to me. I'm the one, from this point, who has the responsibility you speak of. It will make the exercising of that responsibility more straightforward and more effective if you and your shift-crew retire to your quarters and rest until you are called upon to serve once more. Which I strongly suspect will be soon enough."

"But the attack—"

"To clarify," said Yolande, "we are not 'under attack'. There is no evidence of any other vessel, projectile, particle beam, transmission, or force incoming towards us. There has merely been an excursion from the shuttle bay."

"An excursion?" Rodriquez asked.

"Beowulf, I have command," said Chandrasekhar. "I ask that you not continue to provoke distraction to that responsibility. For the moment, please—"

"I have a right to be kept informed—"

"And in due course, you will be. But seeing as we are currently experiencing something of an emergency—"

"Which is why I'm seeking clarification—"

"You'll get it. Due course. Stand down. Yolande, please instruct Beowulf Rodriquez to rem—"

"It's alright, Stef," said Rodriquez, nodding towards Chandrasekhar. "Yolande has made the call, and I'll abide by her decision."

"Not before time—"

"I do not consider that tone appropriate. It's precisely because this is an emergency that I am seeking clarification. I will leave the bridge now. I ask only that I be kept informed, as a courtesy, of any capital decisions undertaken in my absence. Yolande?"

"Of course," Yolande answered. "All necessary details will be included in your next commencement-of-shift briefing pack. As always."

"But I also need to clarify this. Someone went on an outing?"

"That is an unfortunate term, and I regret if a misunderstanding has resulted from its use. I mean, of course, that a craft has left the shuttle bay. It has done so unexpectedly. You will have to excuse me. Ten minutes ago I was not aware we *had* a shuttle bay."

"We've always had a shuttle bay," explained Pernillesdottir, in a patient and reasonable tone. "It's where we keep the shuttles."

"Naturally," replied Yolande. "And I once again have full access to that information. But for some indeterminate period of time preceding that, I did not. It was as though there were an obstacle in my memory. And I do not know the—"

"Do not know the what?" asked Rodriquez, after the silence had stretched for a couple of seconds too long.

As far as communications from Yolande were concerned, it would stretch much longer.

Daycycle 1831 (still)

No living creature more self-aware than a paramecium copes well with emergence from hyperspace, but some manage more poorly than others. Hamdi Kwan, historian, translator of ancient poetry, and sometime mahjong companion of Karinette Lichtermann, was one who, he had just now discovered—thankfully within the confines of his own inconveniently-shaped cabin—was hit especially hard by the process. The two hemispheres of his brain appeared to have filed for separation, his lungs had that freshly-sandpapered feeling that is all well and good for a woodworking project but is not at all what one wants in amongst one's respiratory bronchioles, his eyes were reporting visual disturbances that would likely linger for weeks in his nightmares, and his legs had worked out for themselves some unfathomably complicated roster which detailed, on a moment-by-moment basis, which one of them was to be immobile and lumber-numb and which was to manifest unbearable agony. He had, accordingly, put himself to what he hoped was his bed and was seeking with little prospect of success to reacquaint himself with the phenomenon known by optimists as 'sleep', in the expectation that some of the torment might have abated, or at least relocated, by the time he awoke.

He awoke, with no concept of whether it had been minutes or hours. It appeared, on the basis of mouthfeel, as though it might have been years; but he judged this unlikely. Abatement of any mode of his corporeal suffering was not in evidence, and he could not be sure that the cabin itself was not throbbing. The noise from the ventilation shaft wasn't helping, either. A scraping sound, like a scalpel on bone, and a dreadful thin keening. Perhaps it was a hull breach. He was too sick to care.

But he was not quite too sick to wonder why the hull breach might be calling his name. He sat up, stood, and tottered across to the ventilation grille which, thanks to an unreasonably low ceiling on that side of the room, was inset at shoulder height into the wall. He bent to peer at the grille, rubbing the back of his neck in a futile attempt to forestall complaints from that portion of his anatomy.

There was something in the vent shaft. Something with eyes.

Despite his best intentions, he met its gaze.

For several hours, the situation aboard the *List of Wealthy Donors* grew increasingly desperate. Air circulation and purification, thermo-regulation, fusion reactor control, illumination, shipboard navigation, plumbing and communication had all, at a stroke, become unreliable, and Captain (Third Shift) Chandrasekhar delegated to Captain (Second Shift) Rodriquez the responsibility of assembling a team who would be tasked with urgently bringing these essential services under human control. That Stef Chandrasekhar's motivation for doing so had been, in part, a consequence of her need to get Rodriquez out from under her feet while she took charge on the bridge should not, this narrator strongly feels, go against her: it was the right decision, and Beowulf Rodriquez was the right person for the role. For her own part, placed in command of a vessel that nobody on board yet knew quite how to fly, Chandrasekhar had elected to focus on an attempt to restore Yolande to some semblance of functionality, and the bridge was consequently crammed with shipmind technicians, network specialists, quantum-memory retrievalists and AI distribution analysts, each of whom was talking louder than the next person, in more opaque jargon, and seemingly able to agree only that the smell of frying quantonics emanating from several of the most highly-structured of Yolande's meshware hubs was not at all, in the circumstances, a good smell to find oneself smelling.

"It has to be sabotage," said Engineer (Third Shift) Melia Pernillesdottir, approximately two hours into the shipmind revival effort. "Modern shipminds are designed at such a fractal level of redundancy that there's no chance at all of such a systemic failure occurring by accident. Whoever did this planned it, and planned it carefully."

"Why would anybody do such a thing?" Chandrasekhar asked.

"No idea," replied Pernillesdottir, stepping aside while a technician energetically plugged an unnecessarily talkative meter into the diagnostics port of a rack of memory gel-slabs. Raising her voice, she added, "But I'm also not convinced, notwithstanding the limitations in my own knowledge of shipmind cerebro-networking, that trying to engineer a solution to the problem might not be making the matter worse."

"Say again?"

"I mean that I cannot guarantee that Yolande's attempted revival, however well-intentioned, will not have disastrous effect."

"Damn it, Melia, you know I'm not good with double negatives," said Chandrasekhar, frowning as a tall white-coated individual strove, for some unspecified purpose and without macroscopically measurable success, to move the captain's chair sideways. "Are you saying we should be trying to fix Yolande, or we shouldn't be trying to fix Yolande? Or we should perhaps be tossing a credit token to decide?"

"I'm saying that our best bet is to shut down all power to the circuitry through which Yolande used to operate. In all likelihood, this... well, this shipmind takedown I suppose, is something that was coded for, and if that code is still operative, there's a possibility we could unleash more of it, possibly to devastatingly worse effect. I mean, right now the air smells, the heating can't make up its mind whether to go full pelt or not a sausage, and the bathroom facilities are best avoided by those with sensitive digestions, but we haven't depressurised, or lost containment, or suffered anything instantaneously catastrophic. Bad air can kill us in an hour or two, but an hour or two gives us time to act."

"Can you move your feet, please?" asked the would-be captain's chair repositioner.

Chandrasekhar stretched her legs out horizontally, momentarily contemplated using the technician's back as an ottoman, and turned back to the engineer. "So you're saying we should stop troubleshooting Yolande?"

"That would be my recommendation," said Pernillesdottir. "Captain."

"Yolande?" Karinette asked—the request, after five years aboard, was second nature—as the door chirped once more. There was no response from the shipmind, though a series of further chirps from the door suggested that whoever was waiting in the corridor was strongly interested in seeing her.

"Karinette?" asked the door-muffled voice. Male, though it didn't sound like Gandel Urkhart, nor entirely like Preston Lavoisier. Which, all things considered, was probably a selling point.

"Who's there?" she asked, then thumbed the manual override to open the door before the caller had had an opportunity to respond.

It was Hamdi, looking as though he'd been dragged backwards through a jetball practice session.

"Come in," she told him, then glanced towards his feet, and noticed that he wasn't alone.

The restoration of air-purification functionality throughout the *List of Wealthy Donors* was announced by an unexpectedly forceful gust that pushed like some kind of turbocharged, vapour-phase snow-plough through the ship's corridors and byways.

"Is it wise to be running the equipment at that intensity?" Chandrasekhar asked, moving across to the nav console. She'd just now decided that the placement of the captain's chair, directly beneath the bridge's main vent grille—the privileges of rank, and all that—was not an unmixedly advantageous one. And was that a twig in her hair? She reached up, patted the top of her head. "Aside from questioning whether we actually need the immersive wind-tunnel experience at this stage in the proceedings, it also runs the risk of burnout, surely. Or of hypothermia."

"Engineering assures me the system can take it," replied Rodriquez. "And there are greater risks than burnout. We need to clear out the marginal air as efficiently as possible. Once we've achieved that, we can ramp it back to normal levels. Captain."

"That does seem prudent," allowed Chandrasekhar, offering a curt nod of her head. "Captain." Perhaps they would get through this intact, after all. They'd averted the imminent risk of asphyxiation. It felt good to be extending oneself, applying one's capabilities, meeting actual challenges. She rubbed the sleeve of her tunic. "Temperature control next, I think."

"On it," said Rodriquez, his breath condensing in chill clouds. "Though I'd like to borrow Pernillesdottir, if I may, to head up a small team to add some further redundancy into the air-quality control processing. The more failsafe we can make the essential services, the better."

"Indeed. Yes, I think Melia would be just the person for that."

The stretch of corridor to which Hamdi had led her was, in several respects, entirely nondescript, and yet it filled Karinette with a vague and inexplicable unease. She wanted to be able to say that this sense of unwelcomeness stemmed from her recent re-emergence from hyperspace, but she wasn't sure that was true. It would have helped in this regard had there been a sense of lingering unreality to her standing here, with Hamdi and with this small spindle-limbed, goggle-eyed, mangily-furred creature that seemed to have adopted her colleague, but she couldn't justifiably say that it was so. The situation felt unpredictable, in an entirely distinct way to the unpredictability of the lang lab role-plays through which Yolande had put her and Gandel on something like seventeen hundred occasions over the past five years of the voyage; it wasn't, all up, something with which she felt comfortable.

She didn't know why that should be. She was a frontline worker in the effort to establish direct entity-to-entity communication with whoever or whatever might remain of the race that sent the signal beaming across twenty-six thousand light years to the cradle of humanity. Surely she should be inured to the prospect of meeting the unknown? But now she found herself wondering whether the role-plays' accoutrements—the rubber-costumed interns and the multitudinous bizarro *sturm und drang* linguistic ambushes with which Yolande had confronted her and Gandel— had perhaps anaesthetised her but not inoculated her. She didn't know. All she knew was that the corridor felt wrong, and that Hamdi had brought her here without, himself, apparently knowing why.

She found herself reviewing how much she actually knew about Hamdi. It wasn't much.

It didn't help, either, that they'd encountered no fewer than three security patrols on the short walk from her cabin to this unwelcoming corridor, each of which had taken it upon themselves to inform her, unprompted and without useful further qualification, that the situation was entirely in hand and there was absolutely no need to be concerned.

The small smelly creature—the *potto*, Hamdi had called it; its aroma, to Karinette's undiscerning nostrils, appeared to be equal parts engine oil, decay, and burnt electronics—was shambling its way back and forth along the stretch of corridor, pressing at intervals against the featureless wall of the corridor's convex flank as though searching for something.

"Hamdi," she asked, for perhaps the seventh or ninth time, "what are we doing here?"

The historian merely shrugged, then seemed belatedly to sense that verbiage of some sort was required. "I'm not sure," he replied. "Pansy seems to think it's important."

Pansy, she'd gathered, was the name he applied to the potto. She had no idea why he was indulging it so, nor for that matter why she was indulging him. If it weren't that she remained concerned about walking the corridors alone these days, she would have just left him here and retraced her steps to her cabin.

"Okay," she answered. "Next question: why should whatever Pansy considers to be impor—"

She stopped, mid-word, because with a sharp smell of fur-singe, something had suddenly shifted in the corridor wall. No longer a featureless expanse, it could now be seen to be pockmarked, scratched, and sufficiently dented that she grew concerned that it might possibly be one of the vessel's hull walls. This was a suspicion assisted by the wall's prominent sealed hatchway, which looked decidedly more industrial and airlocky than did most of the *List*'s doors, as though this was a structure actively intended to protect against a vacuum on the other side.

Just beyond the hatchway, the potto had raised itself somewhat awkwardly on its hind legs and was running a bulbous-tipped-but-too-thin finger along the illuminated infoscreen affixed to the wall. Its lips were moving silently as it traced its finger repeatedly across the screen, a centimetre lower each time.

It's reading, she realised with a shock. Before she could wonder further on this development, the hatchway started opening.

Daycycle 1832

She should retreat to her quarters, should get what rest she could. She wasn't serving a useful purpose on the bridge anymore; for now, she was just another obstacle for those on duty, a slumped figure in uniform, barely able to keep her eyes open and relying for lateral support upon a console whose purpose, for the moment, she had forgotten. She really should move. But movement would require effort, and she was spent.

Captain (Third Shift) Stef Chandrasekhar was exhausted, at the cellular level; apprehensive, at the molecular level; and emotionally drained, at the atomic level. To compound matters, there was the strong probability that every further shift she completed would also leave her feeling this way, in this new paradigm wherein Yolande, for so long the *List of Wealthy Donors'* lifeblood and guiding hand, was no longer to be relied upon to maintain shipboard order. The thought terrified her; it also left her with a sense of pride and accomplishment. Command, it turned out, was damned hard work. She and Rodriquez, and their respective shift crews, had done it: they had pulled the vessel back from the edge, they had restored, for now, the moment-to-moment functionality of an almost unimaginably complex machine which, up until a few hours ago, they had taken almost entirely for granted as an autonomous and self-sustaining construct. Rodriquez, who against her directions had insisted on remaining on duty for a full additional shift, must surely have felt even more bone-weary than was she, who had felt it necessary to stay on hand for the hours it had taken to become reassured that the ongoing problems faced by the *List* were manageably within the capabilities of Captain (First Shift) Vlad Styring, on whom she and Rodriquez had occasionally compared notes and had concluded that Styring, however good he might look in the uniform, was perhaps rather more forgetful and altogether more clumsy than was truly desirable in an individual placed in charge of several million tonnes of intricately-assembled technology moving at unimaginable speeds through an abstruse mathematical distortion of deep space. Still, the officers surrounding Styring on his command shift were highly capable individuals, who could surely keep him from inadvertently pressing the wrong button at a crucial moment...

...and Rodriquez would be back on duty, here, on the bridge, in another four hours. She hoped he would be sufficiently refreshed to face whatever unforeseen complications the new shift might hold. She hoped she'd have succeeded in stumbling off to her cabin before then.

The priority, for now, remained survival. It would be a few daycycles yet before the List was sufficiently secure in its operations for those in command to contemplate commencement of the search—necessitated by the chaotic stellar-motion free-for-all that held sway in the star-crowded expanse this close to the Galaxy's centre—for the current position of the stellar system from which the signal had been sent, those twenty-six thousand years ago.

The ship would be ready, soon enough, for whatever encounter might subsequently ensue; but would its occupants?

Stef hauled herself to her feet. It would be best to attempt the short walk to her quarters, and to the hopeful mercy of sleep's temporary oblivion, while she was still capable of movement.

The expanse—the hangar, the shuttle bay, whatever—was ill-lit, its adjoining corridor the sole source of illumination, its further reaches shrouded in sprawling sea-deep shadow. There was, nonetheless, enough light for Karinette to mark the large hall as the scene of an impressive quantum of destruction. Judging by the evidence of the hangar's best-lit subdomain, the entire enormous hall was a mess, a post-electronic-era midden of dismantled shuttles, discarded tools ranging in complexity from Allen keys to self-motivated vacuum welding rigs, feathers, crumpled papers, droppings, oil stains, and sundry pieces of apparatus that showed every sign of having been demolished in unseemly haste. It was, thought Karinette, a dismal sight, its evidence of erstwhile carnage undermining the essential sense of security she'd cultivated for herself these past five years. She, and everyone around her, had traversed an almost unfathomable distance in a vessel which, it was now plain, was and remained dramatically more vulnerable to the forces of desecration than she, and presumably the large majority of her colleagues, crewmates, and fellow travellers, had ever chosen to contemplate. They could die out here, and might quite conceivably never be found. Would the distance make of it a lonely death, when so many of them were present?

The potto sneezed, wiped its nostril on a russet-furred digit, walk-crawled its way over to the nearest of the cavernous hall's three principal mounds of components and junk, the objects which had presumably been, not so long ago, fully-spaceworthy vehicles for the transport of personnel and of small consignments of equipment. The hulked shuttles were approximately aligned along the hangar's long axis, but were not evenly spaced: at the midpoint of the larger gap, approximately ten metres from either of the trashed craft flanking it, the floorspace was conspicuously almost free of the litter strewn elsewhere. There had been a fourth shuttle, plainly; it must have left the ship through that now-sealed hatch *there*, in the far wall, its passage marked by those parallel floor-scrapes *there* and by the messy Rorschach burn-marks on the industrial-ceramic wall beside the hatchway through which she and Hamdi and the inquisitive little animal had entered.

The potto had clambered to the top of what looked like an atmospheric control surface: a tailplane? Clinging to the bulbous extrusion of a running light, it flicked its gaze this way and that, slid down and skittered with frenetic agility across the lower slopes of the mound of metal, ceramic, plastic, and less-definable material that enveloped the junked shuttle. Its eyes met Karinette's for an instant. *It's terrified*, she thought. *Of us? Of what it might find here? Or of what it might not find?*

It was plainly, though, looking for something. Now it was rooting about along the slopes of Heap Number Two.

Daycycle 1855

You'd think two internationally-acclaimed experts in communication would be able to find things to say to each other, mused Karinette, and wondered if she should, indeed, give voice to the thought.

There was a dispiriting sense of estrangement between them. Her intuition told her this was only partly due to the disruption in routine that had been wrought by Yolande's continuing absence, and only partly attributable to the secret Karinette now held, of Sal Hinkley's ill-fated cognitive boosting of a troupe of dangerous and disruptive and mission-derailing pottos. There was something else in there too, something she couldn't put her finger on, something Gandel was holding to himself.

He might well be adept at keeping a secret, but he was useless at concealing the fact he was keeping it.

They'd met for coffee. Things were unexpectedly quiet in the Zero Gravy, though having sampled the alleged coffee Karinette decided it perhaps wasn't so unexpected. She found it difficult to meet Urkhart's gaze: unshaven, unkempt, unwashed and unbuttoned, her colleague appeared to have fallen on hard times. Though with Gandel it was always somewhat difficult to tell.

They no longer did the role-plays. They'd met in the lang lab just once, two daycycles after Yolande's termination: Karinette, Gandel, Ensign McGillivray. It had felt like a wake. Without Yolande's freewheeling xenolinguistic-dungeon-master guidance, the exercise had felt forced and unproductive, and not even the whimsically nostalgic sight of McGillivray reprising her rubber-suited role as the sentient broccoli stalk of sessions 395, 1121 and 1407 had managed to energise the encounter. There was no point in seeking to resurrect the semblance of routine. Without Yolande's guidance, it simply did not hold together.

Gandel was well. Karinette was well. They were each keeping busy. That was all they'd learnt from this meet-up: that, and the knowledge that the Zero Gravy very badly deserved to lose its coffee licence, if indeed it actually held one. She wondered what Gandel was keeping secret, though it wasn't as if she had any genuine need to know. He'd always been prone to an odd, sideways perspective on the machinery of life: the blancmange incident, which now seemed so long ago, was entirely in keeping with an Urkhartian tendency to grasp the wrong end of completely the wrong object that looked like a stick but on closer inspection wasn't. It was always possible that whatever was going on within the dusty and ill-dressed confines of Gandel Urkhart's mind, as he sat opposite Karinette in this misbegotten postmodern shrine to foodborne disease and poor customer service, might once again lead to the kind of pivotal xenolinguistic discovery through which he'd established his reputation; it was possible, but it wasn't probable.

How had it happened? How had she managed to become tethered—in a professional sense only, thank gerund—to such a desiccated has-been of the field, such a triumph of reputation over ability? A face that could double as an advertisement for distressed leather; eyes forever collecting whatever photons made it past the perpetually-grimed lenses of his spectacles, yet never truly *seeing*; a mind as sharp, these days, as a mallet. She tried to work out just what it was she felt for Gandel. It wasn't revulsion, wasn't pity, wasn't contempt—he'd earned none of those—but it was something that shared genetic material with all of those, something in which the dominant ingredients were frustration and disappointment and, somehow, wistfulness that those five years had not been spent with a more effective, more insightful mentor and colleague. It was, all up, a waste.

"We were getting too dashed close," Urkhart said, staring deep into her eyes and giving a wan smile which might equally betoken regretful fondness or constipation.

Karinette gave a startled twitch of the head, frowned. She did that thing where you make your nose do a sit-up, briefly, while you squint in disbelief or sudden caution. "What do you mean?" she asked, unnerved by the confessional tone in his voice, and by the uncanny semantic overlap with the messy conclusion to her most-recent-but-one romantic relationship.

"All the role-plays. We were clearly jolly well getting somewhere. That's obviously why Yolande was terminated, we'd almost cracked it."

"That's not how I see it," said Karinette. "The role-plays were training us in versatility and quick thinking, and I guess learning how to mask or override a sense of physical discomfort, but they were never about actually trying to translate the signal, and I certainly don't feel that we had been making any useful progress in that direction." She pressed the heel of her hand against her forehead, to stave off an incipient coffee-or-at-least-something-that-claimed-to-be-coffee headache. "Besides, I don't think it's fair to say Yolande was terminated. She was more than just a machine; she was, in every important sense, a person. And a friend to me, and many others. She wasn't 'terminated', Gandel. She was murdered."

"Oh, I don't disagree," he replied. "But what I mean is that the past month has given me a lot of time to think these bally matters through. And I think we were getting dashed close to a breakthrough."

"We weren't," she said. It bugged her that he so steadfastly refused to keep anything that could reasonably be called a grip on anything which vaguely approximated reality. There had been no breakthroughs in five years of the role-plays because the role-plays were not about breakthroughs. They were training, nothing more. Valuable, in the sense that the repeated unfamiliarity kept the xenolinguists on their toes; highly worthwhile, as an exercise in finding professional comfort way beyond one's own comfort zone; energising, in some cases, when the process worked. But not insightful, or anything of that flavour.

What irked her most, she decided, was that everything positive she'd ever associated with working with Urkhart had been shown, ultimately, to be contingent on Yolande's participation. It had been Yolande who had seen to their training; and that part of the voyage was now done. She'd felt a part of herself atrophy during the past weeks of forced inactivity, and Gandel sitting across from her now just reminded her of that more forcefully than did his absence.

She became aware that he'd been talking; she'd no recollection of what he'd been saying. She closed her eyes and pinched the bridge of her nose. Breathing through her teeth seemed also to be called for, so she did some of that too. Her head was really getting quite bad. She stood, eliciting a squeal of complaint from the chair. "I'm sorry, Gandel," she said. "My head's throbbing. I've enjoyed catching up, but if you've nothing more to say, I really need to lie down now."

"I do have more to say, though," he replied.

She sat down again. "Oh, alright. Out with it."

"It isn't easy," he began. Paused. Wiped his nose on his sleeve.

"What isn't easy?"

"I've been sure before, and wrong. Now I'm not sure, but I could still jolly well be wrong."

"Dammit Gandel," she snapped. "You're still giving me preamble, when what I want is amble."

"I think the signal, and therefore the signal-senders' fundamental language, or whatever passes for it, might be intrinsically undecipherable because of the absence of any referents in common. I'm firming to the dashed idea that the signal source's proximity to the Galaxy's largest black hole is not a coincidence. I know there's some consideration that black holes might be gateways to other universes. I believe the signal's senders are refugees or castaways or what-have-you from such another universe, forced to jolly well plead for assistance from the locals but constitutionally incapable of communicating comprehensibly with them."

"I know how they feel," said Karinette, pressing her fingertips firmly against her forehead.

"No, but the point is you dashed well couldn't," said Gandel. "You can't. None of us can. They're not like us, in any way. They're not made of atoms. They perhaps don't realise the futility of the attempt, very probably they jolly well don't, else they wouldn't have been persisting with it." He scratched his scalp, seized on something small and particulate which his explorations had uncovered.

Stared at it for a couple of seconds before brushing it away from between his fingers and continuing. "Though then again, that presupposes their bally thought patterns to align with our logic, which they likely wouldn't. We don't know what would make sense for them." He glanced across to her, lifted his smeary spectacles aside. "Don't you see that this jolly well makes sense of our inability to understand the signal's content?"

She meshed her hands together, marshalled her thoughts before replying. *A good academic never replies in haste*, she told herself. "First of all," she began. "Gandel, it's an *alien signal*. Sent by, you know, aliens about whom we frankly know nothing except for their ability to structure and focus an electromagnetic signal. It stands to reason it's not going to be straightforward to decipher. I see no reason to evoke any of this from-another-universe fantasia. There's no evidence, frankly, to suggest they're anything other than of this universe. They communicate using photons, which suggests at least a working knowledge of this universe's physical laws. And for heaven's sake, there have been cases enough of language-based human artefacts which defied straightforward translation. On Earth. From within the historical era. If you want an example of that, just—"

"Please don't bring up the bally Voynich Manuscript again," said Gandel.

"Actually, I was thinking of 'Louie Louie'," replied Karinette. "But since you mention it, Voynich was even *illustrated*, which is such a cheat, and it still took us a couple of hundred years. So it doesn't really bother me that we don't yet know what the signal says. It'll bother me more if that's still the case after we've interacted with the extraterrestrials and observed their body language et cetera. And I have to hope that they'll be trying to meet us halfway, of course."

"They won't jolly well know how to," said Gandel.

"I really don't see where you're coming from. You say you think Yolande was killed—and yes I'm using that word deliberately because that's what happened—because we were in your eyes getting too close to translating the signal, and then literally in the next breath you're saying—"

"Dash it, I mean, you can't say it was literally the next breath," he protested. "That's a shameful abuse of the word."

"No, Gandel, it's what the word means. As you'd know if you paid any attention to idiom and to shifts in linguistic tone over the past eighty years or so. And this business of the signal's senders having popped into existence here from some other universe, I have no idea what wormhole you pulled that out of, but it's... it's arbitrary and unnecessary and it's entirely unsupported by the facts. Occam's Razor—"

"It explains why we've had no success in deciphering the signal."

"You're entitled to think that," she said. "But I happen to reckon you're wrong. And I reckon also the reason you've latched on to this other-universe theory, this late in the daycycle, is that it gives you an out. A reason for why you can't actually deliver the goods when the time comes. You're afraid of failing on this mission, because of the reputational damage you'd suffer, and you have a looming sense that that's what's in store. Well, I won't go along with that. I may well fail every bit as comprehensively as you, but I'm determined to go into that contact scenario believing I can just maybe make a positive difference to the outcome. If you can't assist me in that, then I'm better off without you. Speaking of which… I really do need to rest my head." She rose from her seat, tried to muster a smile suitable for departure. "I'd say it's been good to catch up, but—" She let the sentence drift, turned to go.

"Take care," he said, sounding so genuinely hurt that she felt a shard of remorse. "We must do this again, when you're feeling better."

We must not, she told herself. "Yes, well," she answered. And left.

Daycycle 1856

Under normal circumstances—and you will need, here, to grant this author some licence as to this application of the word 'normal'—the theft of a shuttle, the wanton disassembly of three further shuttles and sundry other items of equipment, the theft of sundry other items of equipment, and the destruction of the *List*'s governing shipmind would all be matters that could be addressed quite satisfactorily through the perseverance of Security's well-resourced investigative unit. But in the initially desperate struggle to maintain the *List*'s habitability post-Yolande, the attention of Adrienne Christofforou-Takahashi and the investigative unit's other officers had been elsewhere: on the distribution of a makeshift network of autonomous air sensors across the vessel, on the rescue of a cabal of off-duty topologists from an inexplicably-locked cafeteria, on the manual dousing of two small corridor fires following the failure of the vessel's sophisticated fire-suppression systems. There were so many facets to the disruption of shipboard safety from the loss of the centralised systems which heretofore had overseen it that, for the first seventy-two hours after Yolande's demise, Adrienne and her colleagues had been as exhausted, as stretched, as dependent on fortune, gut feeling, and instinctive risk aversion as everyone else on board.

It had worked. Three aboard the *List* died during those three daycycles, in circumstances on which hindsight shone its ever-unforgiving light. Their loss was keenly felt, not least by those with direct responsibility for avoiding all such casualties, but it was widely agreed—hindsight notwithstanding—the toll could very easily have been much higher. Imminent disaster had been dodged.

Hindsight bit its tongue. There would be other opportunities, as always.

The restoration of a cautious semblance of some sense of normality, after those few hectic days, was welcome. Now the shuttle incidents and the shipmind's death did indeed receive the attention they merited. Christofforou-Takahashi and the other investigators had ample motivation to pursue the matter with diligence, nigh on a calendar year into the foundered efforts to solve any of the brutal and animalistic slayings that had started with Sal Hinkley's murder. But the team's pursuit of the truth behind the shuttlejacking, and behind Yolande's death, was slow, impeded as it was by the seemingly total failure of surveillance in those arenas. It was difficult, for some time, to get any useful data on surveillance anywhere within the vessel, so inextricably were those data linked to Yolande's severely damaged memory caches. Extraction and perusal of the surveillance records was piecemeal, haphazard, and ultimately unsatisfying: it increasingly seemed that all pertinent traces of the planning and execution of these events were not merely inaccessible, but missing. Erased, or perhaps never gathered.

The physical investigation of the shuttle bay fared little better. It presented, in one sense, a crime scene bearing a wealth of material evidence, but the team's overworked analysts found only wreckage and animal waste, with the latter eluding any positive identification. There were no traces whatsoever of the shuttlejackers. Nor did personnel records offer an indication of who might be responsible. Whoever had taken the shuttle had not returned; but it ultimately became apparent that none were freshly missing from the crew manifest. It beggared belief that, on even so large and disorienting a vessel as the *List of Wealthy Donors*, one or more stowaways might have gone undetected for five full years; it strained credulity that, as one woman claimed, a troupe of small monkey-like creatures had comprehensively vandalised the shuttle bay and had somehow stolen one of its vehicles; also utterly improbable was the assertion that the damage was a set-up, perpetrated by the now conveniently defunct Yolande as some secretly-programmed insurance claim on behalf of the vessel's design and construction consortium. It made rather more sense to hypothesise that one or more individuals from the *List*'s personnel—the supposedly-late Hinkley himself was, in some eyes, a prime suspect—might have gone quietly and then spectacularly rogue, but with sufficient foresight to have painstakingly erased all record of their presence before committing their crimes. But to what purpose? It none of it made sense.

Ultimately, Adrienne and her colleagues were reduced to publicising a call for personnel to come forward if they had any recollection of persons onboard whom they had not seen since the shuttle theft. On a large vessel where people frequently took the wrong turning at an inauspicious corridor junction, or perhaps actively sought to avoid contact with research rivals, there were, it transpired, many such trails. None of them led anywhere.

*

Sleep, that sometimes fickle companion, kept her awake.

It was in part, Karinette thought, the horrendous catch-up session with Gandel that had thrown her out of diurnal equilibrium, though the absence of the erstwhile routine didn't help. The two, of course, were connected.

She tossed. She turned. She drank what the corridor's sustenance-supply bot alleged was warm milk. She fretted, and fulminated, and wondered what she was doing, where she was going. Her late-night lack-of-sleep thoughts preyed on her like mealworms picking clean the skull of one recently past caring that she had bequeathed her body to anatomical research. Could it be said that she had made anything useful of her life? What even was the purpose of sleep, other than as some sort of sensory fast-forward button through an already short existence, and why, therefore, did it so unsettle her that she wasn't getting it? She tossed and turned some more, ignoring the mattress's complaints. The mealworms feasted.

She should, she told herself, get up and do something more useful, in sleep's absence, like sorting her shoes by albedo and specific gravity. Or visiting the *List*'s nightlife sector. Or, for that matter, any of her regular daytime haunts. The library. Crawlspace. The virtual beach. The virtue of living on a starship was that it was always morning for someone, and it would be the people for whom it was morning—or, perhaps, early-to-mid-afternoon—who would now be about their business. She could join them. She could get on with stuff. There was, after all, no good reason to court sleep if sleep were not interested.

Conversely, there wasn't really a point in seizing the day when you couldn't even convince yourself that 'day' was what it was. She was physically tired, but her mind wouldn't sleep. *Terrific*, she thought. *What kind of communication specialist can I be? Now I'm even failing to talk coherently between myselves.*

Myself.

Was I unfair to Gandel?

No. It's reasonable to feel disappointed with someone who, on paper, should have been a major influence on my thinking and my career, but who hasn't been, in any positive sense. The sense of a 'team' between us only worked with Yolande's input. I suppose it's useful to have realised that, now, before we actually get into the contact scenario, but it's still dispiriting.

I should sleep.

Why would he claim that the signal's creators must be from a different universe? That's a Preston Lavoisier level of crazy talk, or at least Preston-lite. It doesn't help anyone.

And how could Gandel ever think that we had been getting close to translating the signal? Why would he claim such a thing? That's not even our job, we have cryptographers and information-theory specialists who do nothing else. Ours is just to understand the aliens: ideally through discourse, but via body language if that's what it takes.

What do they look like?

Will I choke, in the crucial moment, when it turns out they don't actually look like McGillivray in a rubber suit?

What if they do look like McGillivray in a rubber suit?

Why can't I sleep?

What if they are from a different universe?

Or what if he was actually right about the blancmange thing?

I need not to be thinking about this stuff right now. I just need to relax, to unspool...

Maybe I should hit the virtual beach.

Oh, that's right. It's offline, after—

Bloody pottos.

I should sleep.

Pansy had eavesdropped on a sufficiently broad continuum of human behaviour to have a fairly clear understanding of the purpose of shampoo, but that didn't mean she had to like it. Nor did she see why it was necessary, for a product whose role was essentially one step removed from that of detergent, that it impart to her fur a cloying and all-too-pervasive aroma of Hibiscus Honeydew, whatever that might be.

The shampoo had been a mistake, a gesture of weakness on her part to have ever acquiesced to her adopted human's insistence on the process. How would she ever manage to sneak up on prey now, smelling like whatever it was the shampoo made her smell like? The fact that there no longer *was* any prey, with the last of the pigeons having been caught and devoured several sleeps ago, was quite immaterial, it was the principle of the thing, it was a bastardisation of the essence of pottoish identity, it was...

...it was a necessary concession to the circumstances, and not worth dwelling on in the more expansive context of his predicament. She'd been abandoned; discarded; left to wither like a dead branch. Those Pansy had known longest—Beatrix, Sherman, Otto, Dennis, Harry, Gail, even the two-foot, Sal Hinkley—had all deserted her one way or another, whether for death or for something equally irrevocable and mysterious. The humans with whom she'd thrown in her lot, in desperation—the old-time specialist Hamdi and the different-talk expert Karinette—were not what she had hoped: they interacted with her, in Hamdi's case more positively than in Karinette's; but, alike, they did not see her. They saw a pet, a curiosity, a need to apply shampoo...

She had sought out companionship in the only place it had been available, among this strange and clumsy and unnecessarily bulky species that presided over the vehicle in which she'd lived all her intelligent life, and had met further disappointment. She'd approached them in the hope that they might understand, might assist her with what she could not do unaided. That, plainly, had been foolish optimism: she had shown them the shuttle bay, she'd made apparent to them how her species-mates had ransacked the shuttles, had deserted her in the process. (There'd been no need to highlight her own central role in that ransacking.) But the humans, who grasped the extent of the damage within the shuttle bay easily enough, either didn't see what she was asking of them, or did not care.

Had she chosen wrong? Had she been as misguided in her judgement on which humans to approach as in her trust, so badly misplaced, in her fellow pottos? She'd never trusted Beatrix, but as for the rest of them... Had the others mourned her abandonment, whenever they had realised she was not in their midst on the dramatically-modified shuttle, or had it been to them a source of mirth, an amusing trifle? That question would remain forever unanswered, were she unable to elicit the humans' assistance. She would have to try again, after this sleepcycle.

She needed to find that scrap of paper, that cover from the manuscript from which she had originally derived her blueprints, at Beatrix's insistence. Then they'd see. *Then* they'd help her.

They'd just have to.

Over the following daycycles, a sense of order gradually returned to life aboard the *List of Wealthy Donors*. Backups to important and vulnerable shipboard systems were designed, constructed, and tested to ensure failsafe operation of essential services; recruitment and training was undertaken to equip those aboard with the knowledge and experience necessary to keep the vessel adequately crewed at all times in this challenging post-Yolande epoch. The focus gradually shifted from the necessities of survival to the complexities of the mission's final crucial phase.

The longest leg of the voyage had been completed. As per the mission profile, Yolande had delivered the *List* to the precise location within Galactic space from which the signal had originated, twenty-six-thousand-odd years previously. But twenty-six thousand years is a not inconsiderable span of time, even upon a Galactic scale, and the stellar system which had, those many lifetimes ago, occupied this position had long since drifted a score or more light-years away, following a complicated trail through the complexities of the Galactic core's crowded starscape. Terrestrial observations of the target system, at such a vast remove in space and time, were never going to be adequate to reliably predict the target's new location: it would have to be searched for anew, now, and fingerprinted by its size, proper motion, and spectrum.

This process took three months. The star, and its retinue of terrestrial planets, were ultimately identified with ninety-nine point three percent confidence at a distance of twenty-four point three light-years from the ship.

A course was plotted, additional crew trained in the operation of the hyperdrive. Briefings were held with the vessel's numerous expert panels. A sense of anxious expectation pervaded the corridors, quite unlike the cautiously optimistic enthusiasm with which the *List* had departed from Sol system more than five years ago. This, now, was the business end of the mission, the approach to its true purpose. The second hyperspace jump would be a much shorter one, a mere two daycycles plus change. Plenty long enough, nonetheless, for disaster to strike, on a vessel not continually safeguarded by Yolande against the dangers that accompanied traversal of the unfathomable, mathematically obscure dimensions within which hyperflight was constrained.

An end-times mood settled upon the *List*. Bacchanalia was celebrated. Prayer circles were held among the burgeoning ranks of the Ussherists. Jetball matches descended repeatedly into bouts of heedless, needless violence, though this was nothing unusual and indeed surprised only the very newest of spectators or participants. Dispensaries ran out of painkillers of every flavour, despite irrefutable and widely-publicised notifications that analgesia was as minimally effective against the torment of Dimensional Re-emergence Syndrome as was the thoroughly-discredited process of cranial trepanation. The ship's dispensaries also ran out of trepanning drills. Two new and vehemently antagonistic schools of outrageously minimalist art were founded and as quickly abandoned by their progenitors because, after all, what was the point?

The ship jumped.

For two daycycles, plus change, those aboard held, in a strictly figurative sense, their collective breath.

Re-emergence, in all its disorienting, recriminatory, emetic glory followed. As did two further, progressively shorter and more precisely calibrated bursts of hyperflight.

Only then did anybody aboard stop to think that the *List of Wealthy Donors* did not currently contain any flight-capable shuttles with which to broach the atmosphere of the target system's target planet.

Daycycle 1937

Karinette was arguing with her clothes hamper when the door chirped. The hamper had been dissembling for several minutes on the location of her lucky yellow socks; Karinette felt that testable inconsistencies had finally begun to show in the receptacle's highly unsatisfactory narrative of unexplained sock misplacement. She was, as a consequence, irked at the intrusion into her domestic affairs, but the door trilled its insistence.

She bade it open, stared. "Where's your little friend," she said, not even caring to give it the intonation of a question.

"Sleeping," replied Hamdi, taking a half-step back. "Sorry. Is this a bad time? Am I interrupting something?"

"Just an impending crime scene," said Karinette, glowering at the hamper in a manner which clearly betokened unfinished business. She breathed out loudly, turning back to her guest at the door. It was possible her eyes may have rolled a little during the process. "Look, it's fine, Hamdi, I've just— I'm just in a grump right now. Busy day tomorrow and all that. Fair warning. But I know you wouldn't have come to see me if it wasn't something important." Her brow furrowed. "It *is* something important, right?"

"It's about our little friend."

Karinette frowned and exhaled again, more loudly. "Hamdi," she began, her voice containing that finely-calibrated level of disappointment which one customarily offers only to cherished family friends who have belatedly informed one of their deeply-held views on cryptocurrency investment, crystal energies, and the Earth's actual and little-appreciated two-dimensionality. "I don't have the time for this. I only answered the door because I thought you might have something to say about the mission.

No idea if you've heard, but I've somehow been drafted onto the shuttle flight that's hoping to rendezvous with the signal-sending species. I need to be ready to board within twelve hours, I need to upload the latest on the signal-decoding effort to my handheld, I have fourteen solid hours' worth of protocol training I need to retake, and I need to get ten hours of sleep. So if it's all the same to you, I'll skip all the proud-potto-dad stuff."

"They've asked me along on the shuttle flight as well," he said. "Something about wanting to ensure the encounter is recorded from an appropriate historical perspective. This is actually about that. May I come in?"

She noted, now, that he was carrying a flattish shoulder-slung plastileather satchel, monogrammed with the initials 'HK'. "I guess," she replied, and stepped back. "But I hope this won't take long." She moved the hamper unceremoniously off her déshabillé bed to make room, smoothed the cover the best she could, and sat down.

"I'll try to be brief," he assured her, hesitating before finding a spot to sit. He unbuckled the satchel and pulled out a crumpled-looking sheet of plastipaper, which he smoothed out before handing it to her. "Pansy found this in the shuttle bay. The others apparently left it behind."

She cast a dubious eye—or rather two, since her vision was binocular—over the page as she turned it over in her hands. It was scuffed, dog-eared, blotted in places with something she hoped were the faded marks of dried coffee stains. It felt gritty, smelt musty. "This is the title page of an unpublished Kit Warburton," she explained out loud, as though the person requiring the explanation were not, in fact, herself.

"I think it's the last thing she finished before she... died."

"Was killed," corrected Karinette. "Steak-knifed through the left ventricle."

"Well, yes," Hamdi conceded.

"By your little friends. With absolutely no apparent provocation."

"I feel every bit as angry with them, at those killings, as you do."

"You can't possibly know that. And you're hanging around with one of them."

"Pansy assures me she was still deep-frozen when all of that happened, she played no part in any of the killings. They only revived her more-or-less as an afterthought."

"And you take her at her word? Of course she's going to present herself in the best possible light," said Karinette. "Her claiming innocence, and them not around to give their side of the story. So I'm sure that's all very convenient for your little friend. But I don't see—"

"I wish you'd stop calling her that. You're making it sound as though I'm some kind of class traitor or something. Species traitor."

"Aren't you?"

Hamdi sighed, closed his eyes briefly before responding. "I abhor the killings that happened. I can't undo them. I'm just trying to find a way forward. And yes, I do believe Pansy is at least less culpable than the ringleaders. And as a historian I'm obliged to note that a body count of seven, eight if you count Yolande, is very much on the low end of the atrocity scale when two disparate cultures encounter one another for the first time."

"You're defending her," said Karinette, audibly riled. "I get that. You're even defending her murder-spree mates, who've high-tailed it in some bastard Heath Robinson-slash-Rube Goldberg mashup of a hotted-up shuttle, leaving us in the process with a few unsorted piles of high-tech junk from which some gang of flight engineers with a wicked sense of humour have attempted to confabulate a makeshift replacement shuttle that they laughably claim to be airtight and flight-capable, with yours truly dubbed in as one of the lucky guinea pigs chosen to crash-test that claim. And I even get that you might be doing all that pottos' devil's advocacy out of some misguided sense of professionalism, or out of some sort of misplaced affection for the lone remaining representative of a previously-unknown society, and it doesn't actually matter to me which of those explanations is correct. Hamdi, they collectively killed Sal Hinkley, one of my closest friends on board the *List*, and—"

"Pansy says it was just Beatrix that killed Sal."

"Again, very convenient for Pansy. But it's because of the pottos that Sal is dead, and Kit Warburton is dead, and that poor overeager cryptozoologist and the others, and I cannot forgive Pansy for that. Regardless of whether she did it or not. Because of what she *represents*."

"I can understand that, but I think it's a pity you hold to that attitude. Have you heard her speak in the pottos' own language?"

"No."

"I really think you should. I mean, obviously I'm no expert, but—"

"Fascinating as the idea of the pottos' language might be—and I'll concede it's another baseline for nonhuman communication, which has some relevance to deciphering the signal—"

"It's a bit more than that," replied Hamdi. "I really do think you need to hear it. And you need to understand what the manuscript indicates about—"

"Hamdi, I thought I explained, I really don't have a lot of time. I need to get ready for what is likely to be the most noteworthy occasion of my career, and I'm currently not at all prepared for it. Now, I get that the title page to an unpublished manuscript by Kit Warburton is an important artefact which will be tremendously interesting to future historians, and I get that the circumstances by which it fell into your hands are sufficiently surprising that you feel the need to share them with someone, but really—"

"Read the title. Take in what it claims to be about. At least."

"Hamdi, I already did. And I just don't— oh." She stared at the page, as if only now noting the all-caps text, turned it over. She reread the manuscript's title to herself, then the by-line, and a cryogenic sensation propagated down her spine. "Oh." Creased her brow. Had to consciously remind herself how to breathe. "The pottos had this. Oh, shit. Tell me they didn't attempt this. Where's the rest?"

"Not here. Beatrix had it last."

Karinette passed the sheet of paper back to Hamdi, looked up to stare at the blank wall of her quarters. "Oh, fuck." Rubbed her arms. Why this sudden feeling of gooseflesh? "You can't seriously be implying," she said, speaking with a cautious slowness that had always served her well in the most precarious of academic confrontations, "what I think you're implying."

"I can," said Hamdi, softly. His gaze held hers without wavering. "I am."

"This is horrendous."

"Agreed."

"Actually, 'horrendous' comes nowhere close to an adequate description. This is an omnishambles of clusterfucks rolled in a shit sandwich *sans* bread."

"Agreed."

If they actually tried this," she said, "they could have majorly tits-upped the entire mission."

"Agreed."

"Please tell me they didn't try this."

"Hear what Pansy has to say," said Hamdi. "It's much, much worse than you seem to think. Karinette, *what the hell should we do?*"

Daycycle 1937 (cont'd)

Karinette had to raise her voice to make herself heard above the machines' metallic chirrups and bleeps. They'd set out towards his quarters—he had insisted that she needed to hear Pansy's vocalisations for herself—but hadn't covered more than a third of the distance before Karinette decided she'd been pushed too far. Present circumstances had left her short on sleep and long on spleen; she knew what she'd hear from Pansy anyway. Mindful that it wouldn't do for the contact mission's historian and associate xenolinguist to be seen in what she was fairly sure was going to be a fraught argument in a public corridor, she'd directed him into the nearest noise-drenched entertainment space so they could have this out in something approaching privacy.

She remembered this entertainment area as a projection chamber featuring brainwave-responsive light displays, a quiet and seldom-frequented domed space of cascading waves and ribbons of colour. But alongside so many other of the *List*'s VR-heavy public diversions, the Brainitarium had been forced to go distinctly more low-tech following Yolande's deactivation. Now it was difficult, within the space, to conduct an audible conversation above the background noise of several dozen pinball machines. Cold, too, for some reason: her breath fogged the air each time she exhaled. She couldn't see the attraction of pinball at all: it seemed noisy, repetitive, pointless and ultimately unsatisfying, rather like jetball, Pentecostalism, and male-gaze pornography. Still, she supposed that on a ship as large and as heavily populated as the *List of Wealthy Donors*, there were bound to be a few adherents to any pastime, no matter how niche. And on the plus side, nobody in here looked likely to pay her and Hamdi any attention.

That suited her fine.

"I only just realised, really," replied Hamdi, staring, a little lost, at the row of clamorous, neon-garish pinball tables and at the backs of the grunting, gesticulating, button-mashing players. He moved clear as a plainly aggravated woman in bodypaint-fit jeans and a red *I Mate Outside My Myers-Briggs Category* t-shirt thumped her table in angry response to a 'Tilt' warning. "I mean, the penny didn't drop until Pansy showed me the manuscript title page. I think it's what she's been searching for all that time, every time she's snuck away to the shuttle bay."

"Hamdi, you talk as though I have the slightest interest in your little friend's excursions. Let the record state that I don't. Let the record also state that you haven't answered the fricative question, so I'll repeat. How long have you known?"

"Three hours or so."

"Just three hours? That's all?" she asked, unwilling to let go of her anger just yet.

He nodded.

"Have you told anyone else?" she asked, rubbing her forearm in an effort to stave off goosebumps. She'd heard that there were, post-Yolande, pockets of uncomfortable chill or heat within the *List*, but hadn't encountered any for several daycycles. "Urkhart?"

"No. I mean, I checked with Cyan about the manuscript, because I knew she helped out with editing and stuff for her aunt, but you're the only person I've told about... this. Cyan confirmed that it showed all the characteristics of a Warburton draft title page, but she said it wasn't one she'd seen. I lowballed it, even held my thumb over part of the title so she didn't ask any awkward questions in response. Far as I can tell, she doesn't know any of the subtext. Are you suggesting we bring Gandel in on it?"

"Hells no," she said, fighting to resist the distractive clamour of the machines, and beneath that the near-subliminal cascade of small percussive events, as stainless steel balls ricocheted off bumpers and flippers. It had occurred to her there was just sufficient complexity and structure within the implementation of pinball for Yolande to have considered it a proto-language, something to explore within one of the lang lab sessions. That hadn't happened, on any of Karinette's shifts; nonetheless, she found herself wondering how Yolande would have presented it, and which of the multitudinous rubber-and-plastic-appendage xenoform costumes would have been foisted upon the patient and long-suffering McGillivray. She shook her head to dispel the train of thought. "Gandel couldn't deal at all."

He nodded and grimaced in agreement, and she was surprised to note that his reaction annoyed her. Partly it was her anger's afterglow, but there was also a flavour of possessiveness: Urkhart was hers to disparage, not his.

As though she alone had ownership of the only correct grounds on which to belittle her mentor.

"But we do have to tell someone," she said. Paused. She realised that the player on the last game in this row was someone whom she recognised. The jumpsuit helped. Bruise. She turned to face Hamdi, was about to comment, but something about his expression dissuaded her. It really wasn't any of her business. "This is too big for us to sit on. Well, for me to sit on, anyway. I'd be derelict in my duty."

"I guess. Security?"

"I don't think so. Security have their work cut out just trying to not make it worse at a jetball match. Besides, when I reported the pottos as responsible for the shuttle bay—"

"You did *what?*"

"It wasn't right to just sit on it, so I reported it. I don't think they paid it any mind, anyway; at least I've never heard back from them. But I'm thinking someone actually in charge, for this development. Who would be best from among the captains?"

"I'd say Chandrasekhar," said Hamdi, resting his elbow against the inclined glass top of a temporarily-vacant table. He had to lean significantly to do so, stumbling in the process on what Karinette surmised was an inoperative grav-tile. Pulling himself up from the gravitational incongruity, he cast a glance floorward before continuing. "She's the most flexible of thought, the least martial, from what I've heard. If I'm assessing that that's what you're after."

"Yes, it is. But frankly we don't have long to arrange an appointment. We need— wait, Melia can give us an in."

"How can Melia help?"

"Pretty sure she's the engineer on Chandrasekhar's team."

"I never remember those sorts of details," Hamdi admitted, stepping back to bring one foot once again into the domain of the faulty floor tile and almost overbalancing in the process. He gripped the metal edging of the tabletop to steady himself. "But yeah, I think you're right on that. So you think we should tell Melia as well?"

"I don't see a choice. We'd be wrong-footing her if we don't."

"You using this game?" a newcomer asked them. The question emerged in a small cumulonimbus of personal fog, accompanied by the scent of that eyewateringly mentholated cocktail Sal had always been partial to. Polar Orbit, if she recalled correctly. The newcomer glanced in a meaningful way at Hamdi and then at the flashing colours of the pinball machine's scoring panel.

"We're just off," Karinette assured him, stepping clear of the menthol-tainted air. She took a last look at Bruise without really knowing why. Untidy social situations always left her feeling confused. "Best of luck."

"Luck doesn't enter into it," the newcomer asserted, flashing a gold-toothed smile and promptly falling with an awkward thud and an oath as he moved into the spot Hamdi had just vacated.

The corridor, when Karinette reached it with Hamdi, was ringingly quiet.

"Stef," said Melia Pernillesdottir, speaking into the comms-plate beside Chandrasekhar's quarters.

"Melia?" The response sounded scratchy: restoration of audio services had not been a post-Yolande priority. "Has that problem with the reactor reasserted itself?"

Problem with the reactor? Karinette wondered. She slid an inquiring glance at Melia, but the engineer shook her head.

"No, Captain," replied Melia. "I'm just here with two of my friends. They wish to speak with you, on a matter they don't believe can wait until morning." She paused, stared at Hamdi for a few seconds, then at Karinette. Swallowed. Frowned. "I'm inclined to agree with them on that assessment." More seconds passed, with no sound of activity from within. "Though of course I'm deeply regretful of the need to disturb you at this hour."

"Very well." The comms-plate's response did not disguise an evident disgruntlement at the intrusion.

The door slid open.

Captain Stef Chandrasekhar's quarters were revealed to be rectangular, and very sparsely furnished, and ultimately in fact merely an anteroom terminated by a double doorway hinting at the existence of more quarters further within. Following Pernillesdottir's lead, Karinette and Hamdi removed their moccasins before progressing to the far end of the anteroom. The double doors scissored open.

The room beyond, also rectilinear, was larger and furnished by a heavy-looking antique table surrounded by eight of those stylish chairs which promise support but no comfort. One of the chairs was occupied.

Karinette registered the room's occupant in a subliminal sense as she surveyed the room, searching in vain for a bed or for the telltale indications, on a mustard-yellow wall surface, that might mark the concealment of such an item. Did Chandrasekhar never sleep? Her attire suggested that she must. But was it then possible that the woman laid claim, through her rank, to as many as *three* rooms? Such room-allocation profligacy was unprecedented; was almost as unsettling, after more than five years onboard the *List*, as the absence of curves and abundance of right angles on display here. This avant-garde architecture would never catch on...

"Let's keep this brief."

Chandrasekhar was notably more compact than Karinette had expected. Youngish, too. Thin-faced, frizz-haired, thick-browed, and possessed of a scowl which might be habitual or might alternatively have been distilled for this particular situation. It was difficult, within the woman's slight frame, to discern the capacity for command, and the lace-edged lilac nightgown and sequinned bunny slippers did not assist in this endeavour. But her diction, her tone, her steadiness of eye all spoke of a readiness to take charge. "Introductions first, I think. And then an overview, please, Melia."

Melia started her spiel. Karinette, belatedly aware that she'd be up next, found herself stricken with nerves.

The meeting with Chandrasekhar brooked a delay of three weekcycles, ostensibly to allow time for the signal-source planet's inhabitants to make the first move in initiating contact with this strange spacefaring vessel which had suddenly materialised within their system, as was recommended by the ship's resident Xenoprotocol Expertise Committee. But as the daycycles dragged by, no symptoms of technically-advanced life were manifested by the planet: no signals, no detectable traces of any dormant or derelict transmitting dish of the kind which must have been deployed for the signal's original transmission, no indication of vehicles rocketing skyward from the planet's surface or breaking from orbit to rendezvous with the *List of Wealthy Donors*. The analysts responsible for pinpointing this apparently verdant but silent world as the locus from which the signal-sending species had operated, those two hundred and sixty-three centuries ago, began to quietly muse that they might, after all, have been mistaken: it was difficult to be completely sure in any assessment as fraught and high-stakes as this one, and it was not beyond the bounds of possibility that they had erred in their identification of this stellar system as the target. It was also conceivable—xenobiology being the surrealist slipstream frontier science that it was—that in honing in on this particular planet from amongst those in the star's orbital retinue, they had made incorrect assumptions: the range of conditions defining what was now known as the Baby Bear Zone (the term 'Goldilocks Zone' having been dragged into disfavour by militant astrobiologists on the twinned grounds of imprecision and unwarranted anthropocentrism) might not, in fact, hold true for all possible biologies. Debate aboard the *List* raged. Fights broke out (or, as they are known within academic circles, 'symposia') and a general air of despondency and purposelessness set in, as though everyone's preferred jetball teams had simultaneously all lost the Preliminary Provisional Grand Final. (In fact, all jetball bouts during this period had been shelved so as not to be misinterpreted by any monitoring alien species.) A major schism erupted within the ranks of the Ussherists, between those who claimed that the telemetry was now revealing the true face of Heaven from which the Almighty himself would surely shortly emerge, and those who started publicly to question whether all this 4004 BC malarkey might be out by, say, an order of magnitude, which would place any genuine edge to the observable universe a further fourteen or fifteen thousand light-years away.

There was also, inevitably, a degree of querulousness about the initial executive decision to expedite a shuttle mission to the planet; this action was now, sensibly, on hold to allow time for an alien response which appeared to be dragging its pseudopodia, but why had it ever been promulgated in the first place?

Alongside the waiting and the 'vigorous academic debate', it was nonetheless still recognised that if the mountain did not come to Mohammed, then Mohammed would need to get himself a decent pair of boots, an iceaxe, and possibly a Sherpa or two. Consequently, teams worked throughout the three-weekcycle deferment, effecting additional repairs and last-minute improvements to the shuttle in which the contact party would travel, should it be the case that no word continued to be heard from the formerly-so-voluble putative inhabitants of the target world. While all of this activity was sensible or at least comprehensible, it did not explain in any sense the *de facto* house arrest in which Karinette found herself.

It had been explained to Karinette that 'house arrest' was not an appropriate description for her situation: she was not charged with anything, was not accused of anything, was not (after a quite brief if nonetheless thoroughly demeaning Security vetting, throughout which nobody seemed to know exactly what was going on) suspected of anything. Also, of course, the *List* was not a house in the technical legal sense, nor could this appellation apply to any domain within the *List* such as, for argument's sake, her quarters. She was merely in 'involuntary isolation' whilst certain decisions were taken. Hamdi, she gathered, was being treated similarly.

She didn't know, didn't really care, what had happened to Pansy. The small primate might well be at large again in the network of ventilation ducts; might be getting underfoot in the shuttle bay, reminiscing or pondering what could've been; might equally well be caged somewhere.

It didn't matter what they called it; it *felt* to Karinette like house arrest. It permitted her darker musings—thrown as they had been, by Hamdi's revelations, into high gear—altogether too much rein to fester. (If indeed that was something of which musings were capable, or which was allowed by an excess of rein.) Cut off from her habitual contacts and restricted to a maximum of thirty minutes of carefully-curated comms conversation daily with Hamdi or Melia, Karinette wondered if she were going quietly crazy; wondered, on occasion, whether her not-entirely-rational arguments with the furniture, or her soliloquys on the iniquity and fundamental duplicity of intellect-enhanced pottos, were disturbing the rest or relaxation of those whose quarters abutted her own. Or perhaps those quarters had been requisitioned for the Security personnel who now appeared (from what she could see, on the infrequent occasions when she opened her door for meal deliveries) to be guarding her corridor on rotation.

She was fairly certain that what was being practised, or at least attempted, was containment: not just of her, and of Hamdi, but of the exceedingly inconvenient information which Hamdi had uncovered. She also suspected, based upon the unrequested preponderance of chicken soup in her meal deliveries of late, that the cover story in circulation to explain her confinement was that she, and presumably Hamdi also, had somehow contracted some highly-contagious illness, and had accordingly been placed in quarantine during convalescence. She did not know what they hoped to achieve by this containment, did not know how coarse or fine a mesh they might be applying for the purpose, did not even know who 'they' were, aside from Chandrasekhar and Melia. She wondered if she had been wrong in insisting to Hamdi that they needed to report what they knew of what the pottos had wrought; but how could they have sat on that information? How could she have gone through with the contact mission, knowing what she did, and keeping it secret? As it was, she fully expected that the mission might yet be scrapped rather than merely deferred, or at the least that she (and probably Hamdi also) would lose their spots on the shuttle flight. She anticipated confirmation of this cancellation each time her door-chime was activated. Yet when word finally came, after three weeks' seclusion, that Captain (Third Shift) Chandrasekhar wished to consult once more with Dr Lichtermann, the news was not this.

Against all expectation, Karinette and Hamdi were still on the mission. Indeed, it seemed that the only personnel change was that Melia's place as first officer and pilot of the contact mission's shuttle craft had been given over to another. Chandrasekhar refused to divulge the rationale for this, refused also to entertain any questions as to how far across and throughout the web of command the knowledge of the pottos' activity might have propagated.

Hamdi appeared content with this, seemed to consider that he and Karinette had discharged all responsibility for the information they had conveyed to Chandrasekhar. But Karinette wasn't so sure. The pottos' treachery carried far deeper implications for her than they did for him. How was she to go through with this, and to maintain a sense of professionalism in a potentially front-facing role? She did not even know whether Urkhart had been informed, could not decide whether it was worse if he had been, or had been kept ignorant.

Daycycle 1959

There are numerous recipes for the forms of conceptualisation required to properly appreciate the sheer immensity of the Universe. But there is arguably no other process that distils this understanding so cogently as to voluntarily find oneself at the pointy end of a lengthy supra-lightspeed traversal of a vast sprawl of Galactic real estate, within the cramped and stale-aired crew compartment of a short-haul personnel shuttle some twenty-six thousand light years on from the second-closest rescue vessel, and to know within one's marrow that such a distance is tiny on a cosmic scale.

The design brief for the *List of Wealthy Donors*' shuttles had stipulated a fleet of four three-person vessels, state-of-the-art but not independently hyperspace-capable. Since no characteristics of the signal-senders' habitat—be it a planetary body, a Dyson shell, a hollowed moon, a free-floating space colony, or a city ensconced within a colossal airtight cavity within the cosmic-ray-raddled corpse of a giant mutant starwhale—were known at the time of the *List*'s departure from the solar system, the shuttles had been designed for trouble-free operation under a wide variety of conditions, as at home in the stingingly cold depths of interstellar space as in the hyperbaric furnace of Venus's atmosphere.

Appropriately, Karinette Lichtermann could also be said to be exactly as at home in the stingingly cold depths of interstellar space as in the hyperbaric furnace of Venus's atmosphere. Which was to say, not at all. Which was to say, she had never previously considered herself to be prone to claustrophobia, but she now found herself wondering whether there were a mailing list through which she could subscribe—or better yet, unsubscribe—to such a service. It mattered not one whit to her what conditions outside the shuttle *Bob's Budget Hovercar Repairs* were like: conditions inside the shuttle were hellish.

It is perhaps instructive, at this stage, to examine the principal factors informing Dr Lichtermann's suboptimal shuttle experience. Firstly, though the designers had fully understood the requirement for a three-person shuttle, they had evidently lacked any comprehension of the concept of personal space. (This is apparently a common feature in the planning and design of pioneering space vehicles.) Secondly, the shuttle had categorically not been designed for easy or effective reconstruction following destructive disassembly and ransacking for parts by small arboreal primates—again, a reasonably common failing of spacecraft architecture—with the result that whatever interior space had existed within the shuttle was additionally obtruded by makeshift replacement componentry which was inevitably more bulky and knobbly than had been the original parts. Thirdly, there were five people aboard. The *Bob's Budget Hovercar Repairs* was, in short, telephone-booth-orgy crowded. Karinette fervently hoped nobody would need to sneeze.

Actually, 'five people' was a slight underestimate, but for excluded-volume purposes the potto Pansy hardly counted. (On Chandrasekhar's express instruction, Hamdi had brought the creature onboard in one of those small hard-case pet carriers.) Karinette, who could feel with every inward breath the handle of the pet carrier pressing against her stomach like some unyielding carbon-fibre third-trimester baby bump, wondered what might be going through the potto's mind right now. Did she appreciate the precious litres of breathing-space afforded to her by the carrier's rigidity? Was she apprehensive about the flight, or about its destination? Did she fully understand what lay ahead, on the planet towards which the shuttle was currently heading? The xenolinguist suspected that she must; and yet it was difficult to tally such comprehension with the small flight-bedraggled occupant of the pet carrier.

The flight was long and was possessed, to Karinette's mind, of an uncomfortable granularity. The nineteen-hundred-day voyage on the *List of Wealthy Donors* had felt, with no overt external markers of movement, less like an unfathomably far-flying journey and more like an unreasonably long and imperfectly-organised conference in some large and decidedly surrealistic hotel: Karinette's day-to-day life aboard the *List* had been, for the most part, comfortable and necessarily monotonous. Work, eat, unwind, sleep. Aboard the shuttle, there was none of the *List*'s illusion of housefly-in-aspic status—the occasional (and, so far as she could establish, undiagnosed) juddering saw to that—but, from where she was wedged, there was also little to suggest actual forward progress towards their still-mysterious destination. If the shuttle felt like anything she'd experienced previously, then, sans overcrowding and with the imaginary addition of some bombastic subsonics-heavy soundtrack and the requisite flashy visuals, it suggested one of those theme-park chambers equipped with hydraulics and actuators to buffet the patrons into believing they were participating in some thrilling interplanetary dogfight. Except, of course, that theme-park ride durations are as short as their designers can get away with, while the *Bob's Budget Hovercar Repairs* was taking an inordinately long time to get to where it was going.

To distract herself from her own thoughts, she pondered the likely thought processes and states of mind of her fellow passengers. Gandel Urkhart she could scarcely be bothered with. If her experience at his side throughout countless Yolande-led role-plays counted for anything, he was probably off on some vainglorious xenolinguistic windmill-tilting daydream in which he played the part of iconoclastic savant-interpreter. Hamdi Kwan would be focussed, most likely, on the implications of the next several hours for the big historical picture. He would be trying, though, to remain at ease, likely with greater success than Karinette herself; she envied the abundant reserves of stoicism and general calmness he seemed to have on store.

Stef Chandrasekhar was less of a known quantity, despite the acquaintance of the past three weeks: Captain Chandrasekhar had that high-command air about her that was a blend of approachability and standoffishness. There was a superficially friendly, almost jovial manner to her, but one sensed that it was not entirely acceptable to press beyond that. In consequence, Karinette felt as though she knew less about Chandrasekhar through direct contact than she did in the context of Melia Pernillesdottir's infrequent workplace kvetching at mahjong. Melia's observations of the Captain's character weren't unmixedly positive, nor did Karinette view Chandrasekhar with any especial fondness after the unasked-for experience of twenty daycycles in unexplained lockdown. Nonetheless, she had no reason to doubt the Captain's competence in this immediate situation: the woman seemed gruff, and on edge, but she had made a point of sounding out the mindsets of her crewmates at reasonably regular intervals and was in frequent communication with her pilot. The edginess might well have been a measure of self-doubt over whatever handling she had done of the potto matter over the past three weeks: there were still numerous ways in which this mission could go awry, whatever procedures, safeguards, and disclosures Chandrasekhar had put in place. Or perhaps she was simply a nervous flier when it came to hastily-repaired shuttles journeying to a destination marked by unknown hazards.

Of all of them, Karinette thought, it was Elvine Laramie, pilot, who was most relaxed at her station. But then Laramie—a short and broad-faced woman with a recently-shaven head now fuzzed by blue-black stubble— was the only one aboard who really had active duties to perform during the flight to their still-mysterious destination. The Captain asked questions but largely kept out of Laramie's way; the others just waited for the flight to be over, probably without any real grasp of why it was that the *List* had not itself approached closer to the target planet. Bla bla security, bla bla quarantine considerations, bla bla hope of concealment, bla bla importance of not placing vital personnel within harm's way unnecessarily. As though any race capable of transmitting an almost pencil-slender radio signal halfway towards the Galaxy's outer rim were not equal, should they put their mind to it, to the task of pre-emptively neutralising a large and largely defenceless space vessel from a distance of half a million kilometres or so. But it was well, of course, not to dwell on such matters at a time like this.

Which, in turn, was a pretty bloody stupid expression. Had there ever previously been a time like this? Even the question made her feel queasy.

The *Bob's Budget Hovercar Repairs* had been enroute for five hours and twelve minutes so far. Which meant another seven minutes since Karinette had previously checked her chrono. She'd heard a suggestion, she thought, that the flight from the *List* was expected to last seventeen hours, 'as long as the fuel gauge readings are accurate'. She didn't like to think of what it might mean if the readings were not accurate. Or if anything else about the shuttle was not as its repairers—still all notably and vexatiously safe aboard the *List of Wealthy Donors*—had judged it to be before signing off on its spaceworthiness.

"I'm getting an update on the *List*'s telemetry of the planet, triangulating from our own measurements," Laramie drawled, reading from the screen. "Surface gravity is 1.2 g, so slightly larger than Earth's. Radius—can you move your head, please, Captain? Thank you—radius is confirmed as also significantly larger than Earth's, by a factor of one point three, so I'd say, comparing that with the g value, it means there's less core, more mantle. That's actually a bit unexpected, this close to the Galaxy's centre. Negligible orbital eccentricity, ditto axial tilt. We'll get further refinements of those data, and others, as the *Bob's* draws closer."

Clearly, Karinette thought to herself, *going by those comments on planetary structure, there's more to this Laramie than just piloting*. This was comforting in some sense, though she wasn't sure why. Perhaps it hinted that the selection process for crewing the shuttle had been a considered and a thorough one, after all?

She still wasn't sure that her own place on board didn't belie that.

"Any sign of habitation?" Stef Chandrasekhar asked.

Just our luck, Karinette thought, *if it turns out we're approaching the wrong planet. Or in the wrong system.*

Laramie turned so as to view the display screen on the opposite wall. The action induced a kind of Mexican body wave that propagated, in sequence, through each of the *Bob's Budget Hovercar Repairs'* sardine-crammed passengers. "No signs of life at this stage, Captain," she said. "That is to say, no direct signs."

"Meaning what?"

"The atmosphere's oxygenated. That doesn't guarantee life, there are some abiologic processes that could also give rise to an atmosphere so sharply shifted from chemical equilibrium, but it's a fairly strong indication. The planet's life-bearing, or was in its very recent past."

"When do we land?" asked Urkhart, who was lodged between Hamdi and the airlock emergency release handle in a way that looked neither comfortable nor entirely conducive to passenger safety.

"We don't," replied the captain. "Pernillesdottir, my chief engineer, vetoed the idea of re-attaching the landing skids. She judged that, with the additional hull strengthening that would have been required, the shuttle could not be made habitable by any crew larger than a mongoose."

It's scarcely habitable now, thought Karinette, then chided herself for uncharitability. It was, after all, an unimaginable honour to have been placed at the linguistics helm for the first ever face-to-face with representatives of an alien civilisation... however devalued the occasion might have been by the developments that had led to that alien civilisation in the first place. *That doesn't matter,* she told herself, not without some difficulty in suppressing some awkwardness. *They are a bona fide extraterrestrial civilisation, and they've had twenty-six thousand years to find their identity as a species. Assuming they haven't all wiped themselves out, and all we end up visiting is the smoking husk of a dead planet. But Laramie said—*

"I'm hardly the expert," said Urkhart, with a tone of barely-repressed frustration that Karinette knew stemmed from his current inability to make expansive hand gestures as he expounded, "but won't that make this little sortie a little dashed, ah, anticlimactic? I mean to say, the whole jolly point of a meet-and-greet is that we do actually get to meet these bally creatures. So as to greet them."

"These people," corrected Karinette, almost reflexively. "The contact species are people. That's a matter of definition. Regardless of what they look like"—she felt herself colouring up—"and it's Pluto to a slurpee they will not look like us... in order for constructive two-way communication to be established with them, wherever that might lead, we have to think of them, and to treat them, as people." *Fine words, K,* she told herself. *Pity you don't even believe them yourself.* It was a little discomfiting to realise that it was antipathy to her colleague, rather than any finer sentiment or desire for academic precision and due objectivity, which had spurred her response.

"It takes two to tango," Hamdi commented.

Chandrasekhar cleared her throat. "As to the lack of a planetary descent capability, it shouldn't be necessary. We expect them to be a spacefaring species; we can meet them in space."

"Isn't that a tad presumptuous?" asked Urkhart.

"I'd say it would be presumptuous, not to say intrusive, on our part to believe we would be permitted to descend to their planet's surface," replied Chandrasekhar. "There are also non-negligible concerns relating to biohazards. On both sides, for that matter, I shouldn't wonder."

"Biohazards?" Urkhart asked.

"Indeed," said Chandrasekhar as calmly as if she were reporting a minor flight correction. "Rest assured that, should we contract anything that appears to be virulent from these, ah, people, we would not be permitted to rejoin the *List of Wealthy Donors* at the end of all this."

"But we might not be able to survive on that planet's surface," said Urkhart. The attempted gesture accompanying his remonstration kicked off something like a Busby Berkeley number as performed by interlocking Escher characters, and it was several seconds before he could audibly voice his next sentence. "Even if the aliens allowed us to stay. And this shuttle can't support us for any extended period of time. We'd need food, and shelter, and water, and medical attention, and... and air. We'd jolly well die."

"Quite possibly so," said Chandrasekhar.

"I do think this might have been explained to me before I boarded," complained Urkhart.

Daycycle 1959 (cont'd)

Pansy was impatient for arrival, whatever that might look like. The impatience stemmed largely from the sense of uncertainty that had held her captive ever since the other pottos' escape. She had not felt secure, had not felt in any sense as though she belonged anywhere, in all that time.

The isolation slammed into her, once again, hitting her like the ground after a long fall. The fruit she'd glimpsed, high above, would be forever out of reach. Each memory of its sighting would only bring pain.

"What's in the pet container?" Gandel asked, seemingly only now noticing the hard-cased intrusion that had been pressing into his calves since the voyage's outset.

"Potto," said Karinette, not meeting his gaze.

"And what's a potto?"

A ghost-eyed, insect-chomping, long-fingered tree ornament with actionable views on personal property, thought Karinette. "A small arboreal primate of African origin."

"That from Sal's dashed petting-zoo idea?"

Karinette nodded.

"Nice to see some inclusion of Hinks's legacy in the contact mission," commented Gandel.

"Indeed," said Karinette, squirming inwardly. *If you only knew.*

He squinted at the pet carrier's ventilation grille. "Couldn't you have jolly well brought something a little more... fubsy? Like a lamb? Or like geese? Everybody likes geese."

"Nobody likes geese," explained Karinette. "And this was what was to hand."

"Wasn't it pottos that—" Gandel began.

"Got something onscreen," Laramie announced, and the others would have all clustered around her if they weren't already unavoidably doing so.

"Station of some kind, orbital, looks to be geo— hold on, I'll magnify."

Try as she might, there wasn't leeway for Karinette to turn sufficiently to view whatever screen was running the telemetry, but she was very grateful of the change in subject. If it had been up to her, she'd have left Pansy behind on the *List*, but Hamdi had insisted. Said that posterity would hold a strong view on the matter. It irked Karinette that the rational side of her brain could see his point.

"Size?" asked Gandel.

"Distance?" asked Chandrasekhar.

"It's orbiting the planet at around forty-five thousand kay," Laramie informed them. "Still trying to get a decent measurement of its dimensions; we're still eleven hours or so from a rendezvous." Pause. "That is, Captain, if you wish to authorise such an action."

"Do it," Chandrasekhar instructed. "Are there... any indications of activity from it?"

"No movement visible at this distance," answered Laramie. "But it's emitting. I can't tell, yet, whether it's actively signalling us, but I am detecting radio traffic."

The news was met by what probably would have been a collective sigh, if space aboard the *Bob's Budget Hovercar Repairs* had sufficed for such a response. As it was, Karinette could sense the pulse of anticipation that propagated through the shuttle's crew. They had a destination, an end goal.

"So what happens," Gandel asked, "when we reach this station?"

"We dock," said Chandrasekhar.

"We can try," said Laramie. "Though it's Betelgeuse to a candle they won't have compatible fittings."

Daycycle 1960

As it transpired, the structure that Laramie had sighted was not an orbital, but a skyhook: a space elevator. The *Bob's Budget Hovercar Repairs* matched orbital velocity and hove to, a few kilometres adrift of the large and near-featureless platform that marked the elevator's geostationary sweet spot, the altitude at which orbital angular momentum precisely balanced both the pull of the planet's gravity and its rotation rate.

Chandrasekhar and Laramie were deep in discussion as to how to transfer the shuttle's crew to the platform when the alien object effectively pre-empted human action. A wide glowing serpentine form emanated from the platform and efficiently sidled its insubstantial way towards the shuttle, making contact noiselessly. An auroral greenish glow blanketed the vessel's internal surfaces, including its occupants.

"Status update," said Chandrasekhar.

"Your guess as good as mine," replied Laramie. "Captain," she added. "No sign of any welcoming party, though."

"It's an umbilicus," said Karinette, squinting in an effort to see more clearly through the nimbus of luminosity. "My guess is they're providing a means for us to get across to the platform."

"It's pulsing," said Laramie. "And Dr Lichtermann's correct about it connecting us to the station, but I can see through it—to a degree, at least. Captain, it would appear to be a force field. It's not composed of matter, at any rate."

"Can we use it to get across?" Hamdi asked.

"Do we have spacesuits?" Gandel asked.

"No room. It was either spacesuits or mission specialists," Laramie said. "We chose to believe the mission specialists might be more useful."

"We have to trust them," said Chandrasekar. "Very well, prepare to disembark."

"Breathable," said Laramie, perusing what Karinette presumed was an airlock monitor of some description. "Kilopascals are about right too."

"We could have saved space on the airlock after all," Chandrasekhar commented, and Laramie laughed at what Karinette had to presume was some sort of private joke between the officers. "Okay, seal the outer lock again. Let's put this umbilicus to the test. Captain's privilege."

Say what you might about Chandrasekhar, Karinette thought as the Captain opened the inner lock and stepped through, closing the hatch behind her, *the woman has guts.*

Constructed upon the platform, there was a room of sorts, which presently held Karinette, and Gandel, and Hamdi carrying the potto carrier, and Captain Chandrasekhar within what seemed like the minimal-effort architecture. The room's ceiling was awkwardly low, but the air stayed breathable, the pressure adequate, the temperature not uncomfortably warm. Light levels were neither too dim for facial recognition nor too bright for comfort, though the light's source was not apparent. There was also a sensation of slightly stronger than terrestrial gravity, which as much as anything spoke of advanced technological achievement, for the room featured neither floor nor walls of any description; just the ceiling and a slender pillar at each corner, the lot of it composed of some hazy insubstantiality. It was not at all clear what was holding the air in place. For all Karinette knew, it might as well be peer pressure.

The view was both awe-inspiring and intensely unsettling. The globe beneath them, blue-skinned by atmosphere, was skeined in a myriad broadly co-aligned fingers of green. Laramie, who had remained at the shuttle's controls, reported that the coloration was due to vegetation, in tall stands, banded by narrow blue-grey seas.

A world of forests and waterways.

Karinette shifted her focus from the sunlit flank to the dark expanse that slowly grew as the elevator platform swung, with the planet, towards night. There were sporadic flashes visible: blue, green, yellow, most easily seen peripherally.

The planet was so strongly Earthlike in its general appearance that it only slowly dawned on Karinette that a part of what she found unsettling about it was its obstinate refusal to yield coastlines familiar from terrestrial cartography. The eye sought Australia, Africa, North and South America, but did not find them on a globe that strongly looked as though it should contain them: a sort of planetary uncanny valley, or the like.

Directly beneath them, there was a small circle of light. Unlike the flashes in the nightside forest, it was static, and it was only after several minutes that Karinette became convinced it was growing. It had not, at first, been so pronounced.

Something was rising to meet the platform.

Daycycle 1960 (cont'd)

An elevator capsule rose untroubled through the whatever-it-was-that-wasn't-a-floor-but-was-nonetheless-not-letting-the-air-fall-out and then stopped. An opening appeared in the capsule's nebulous wall.

Karinette was relieved to see that the capsule possessed opacified and ostensibly solid caps atop and beneath it, but this appeared to be the sole concession towards passenger peace of mind. She was chagrined at its size: it was barely wide enough for one standing human. *A stand-up tubular coffin,* she thought to herself. Then tried, unsuccessfully, to unthink it.

"This is problematic," announced Chandrasekhar. "Every contact scenario I've workshopped had a team of us meeting our hosts. The linguists, a historian, an authority figure. Do we wait for more capsules to ascend?"

"None others visibly approaching, Captain," Laramie reported from the shuttle.

"They surely can't expect us to send one person alone to make contact with a race none of us have ever seen," said Urkhart.

There's not a dramatic lot of difference, Karinette thought, *between sending one person and five.*

"We can't send it back empty," said Hamdi. "Do we just ignore it, and hope they get the message?"

"There's no telling what message they'd get from that," said Urkhart. "But I can list a couple of thousand possibilities."

"Plainly, we need to send a representative to them," said Chandrasekar. "We have to assume they know enough about our physiology to ensure that representative's physical safety."

"They've kept us alive here on this platform," Hamdi noted. "So presumably they have some sense of our requirements. But who should we send?"

"Whom," noted Karinette and Gandel in unison.

"Captain's prerogative," said Chandrasekhar. "I should be the one to place myself in greatest danger; I cannot ask any member of my crew to do more than I myself am willing to do. But I very much think, from an entirely pragmatic perspective, the contact needs to be initiated by a linguist. We need to establish communication, after all, before anything else can ensue. Professor Urkhart, do you accept the honour and the responsibility?"

Gandel had chosen this moment to clean his spectacle lenses with a moistened fingertip. "Send Karinette," he said, looking up briefly. "She was always much quicker on the uptake, in our simulations."

"Our protocols would recommend that the honour be accorded on the basis of seniority," said Chandrasekhar. "And thus to you, as the mission's ranking xenolinguist. This is a unique occasion, of unprecedented significance."

"Yes," said Gandel, as blithely as though delivering a takeaway order. "So send Karinette."

"I—" Karinette began, but really, there was nothing useful to add. Whether this was unparalleled opportunity or another iteration of poisoned chalice, there was no real way to refuse this, not if she wished to maintain any sort of professional credibility. This was what she had trained for. She couldn't turn it down. "I'll take the potto," she added, forcing the words past the throat-lump which had formed on hearing Gandel's unexpected if offhanded endorsement of her capabilities. She picked up the pet carrier from where Hamdi had placed it in the corner. "If there's room."

There was room. Just.

The descent was slow. Karinette did not object to that, because she was not in any sense looking forward to what would follow on her arrival.

Instead, she reflected on what she'd learnt those three weeks ago, when Hamdi had come to her cabin with his disturbing revelations.

She had felt cheated when first she'd learnt of the manner in which they'd all been played: cheated, and cheapened, and undermined. Those feelings had festered; prospered; threatened to invade her core like one of those parasitic brain-infiltrating fungal infections that are reputedly the scourge of certain species of ants. Karinette wasn't entirely sure why this overshadowing mental incursion hadn't indeed happened, hadn't utterly subsumed her; perhaps, paradoxically, it was the supreme sense of disorientation that Hamdi's revelation had induced in her which provided some unexpected grounding.

The elevator capsule continued its descent, now in full night.

Daycycle 1961

When a people have the time, and the freedom, to work out who they are, then they will work out who they are.

This statement sounds mundane, which perhaps it is. Trite, which perhaps it is. Self-evident, which perhaps it is. And yet it is always important—in fact, it is crucial—that this process of societal self-discovery and self-invention happens.

Often, this development involves isolation, argument, conflict, a period of confusion, exploration of alternatives, consensus. Sometimes it is sparked by rebellion, or by cataclysm, or by simple opportunity. There are no maps, no rules, no all-encompassing guidelines for the process, which is intrinsically organic and distinct for every people. Therefore, it is generally not possible to predict how long the process is likely to take; but it is fair to say that a few months, as humans measure it, would be almost certainly insufficient, while a somewhat longer span of, say, twenty-six-thousand-three-hundred-odd years would for most societies be ample to establish a people's sense of self-identity. This is how history happens.

Those aboard the *List of Wealthy Donors* had spent over five years onboard. Long enough, within the bounds of confinement, routine, and common cause, to have established a culture, but not enough time to have become a distinct society, with a sense of destiny properly separate from that conferred on them by the peoples of Earth. That process, were it to have occurred, would have taken a voyage of a century or more: people would need to be born, to live their lives, to die, before it could have been said that the ship's occupants were truly an entity in their own right. Yolande's erasure, too, had hindered or at least diverted the process: those who remained in her wake were changed from their former selves.

If the process of settling upon some form of societal consensus of identity could be expected to take many years, the timescale for the analogous process within an individual human was generally necessarily much shorter, since people by-and-large do not have much more than a century at their disposal. Karinette would normally have said that she had, more than a decade ago, identified the principal values and characteristics which she considered self-defining, the rules by which she would proceed to live her life; now, here, with the orderly expectation of promotion, occasional achievement, incremental academic process, and eventual quiet retirement thrown into doubt and faced with an unknown and inherently unpredictable future, she wondered if this were so. She had had insufficient time since the upheaval imposed by Hamdi's revelations to have sorted out for herself her niche in all of this. She was still quietly furious at the creatures who had brought about the deaths of Sal and Yolande and the others, but she was trying to maintain a professional's focussed calm. Anger had no place in a first-contact scenario. Nor, for that matter, did resentment, or personal grievance; but how could she rise above those, and not feel a sense of disloyalty?

Karinette envied the detachment and acceptance that Hamdi had been able to show; perhaps that was one of the attributes that came more naturally to historians than those in other, less-long-view occupations. Or maybe it said more about his personality than his profession.

Perhaps he should have been the first one to ride down to the surface, she mused. *With his little friend and his capacity to let bygones be something to calmly pick apart in publication after publication.*

Or maybe it should have been Gandel. And not just on a seniority basis. Gandel doesn't have the baggage I have, about Sal and the pottos. That is, he has plenty of Sal-shaped baggage of his own—at least, I have to assume that's the case, though he never says anything about that—but he's ignorant of the potto connection, so in that sense he'd be more objective. Feathery, sure, and probably cackhanded as all hell, but fair about it.

But that, too, would've been a copout, on my part. No, this is on me. Though gerund only knows why that should be the case.

How the hell do I do this?

If Pansy, riding in the pet carrier, sensed the antipathy within the slow-burn internal conflict that was Karinette's present emotional state, she didn't show it. Perhaps the acquisition of intellect blunted the native ability of animals to sense hazards such as fear or anger, or perhaps Karinette herself were simply inept at reading intelli-potto body language. Perhaps, given that she would shortly become the first human emissary in history to ever encounter the representatives of an established and technologically advanced extraterrestrial society, her thoughts would be better directed outwards than towards the vagaries of her own mental state. But it was difficult: the cylindrical wall of the elevator car had unhurriedly opacified, perhaps to match the capsule's ceiling or perhaps as a defence against unfiltered sunlight, which ensured that, regardless of which direction she turned, she was met by her stretched, lit-from-below reflection; she did not care to scrutinise the now-transparent floor, which revealed altogether too much alien real estate at altogether too high, still, an altitude. There was not even the dubious benefit that would have been conferred by the presence of alien muzak.

She was not ready for this, but she needed to be.

Had she done this before?

Had this... this hijacking of reality happened repeatedly? Hundreds, thousands, millions of times, jolting back and then inching forward in time, repeating itself perfectly (or perhaps not so perfectly) on each closely-overlapping occasion? Was she merely one small spindle-turning cogwheel affixed at some seemingly arbitrary point along an almost incomprehensibly long and complicated chain of causality that looped around to meet itself like some monstrously large drive belt or like the legendary tail-nomming worm Ouroboros? Was she even a cogwheel? Would she feel put out if it transpired that she were not, in fact, a cogwheel? Was she courting disaster by, at this very instant, contemplating cogwheelhood and all it might entail, as she now fell towards night on a carefully-landscaped alien planet? What, exactly, was expected of her? Was anything expected of her? What did she expect, or what should she expect? How could it all *be*?

There must have been a signal to begin with, the whole thing could not simply have materialised out of quantum nothingness and rounding errors like some sort of primordial universe. And that initial signal must indeed have originated from the Galactic centre, or at least from along the line of sight that, passing through the Galactic centre, intersected the Earth. There was, after all, a lot of Galaxy further along that line of sight, a lot of hinterland real estate. Perhaps the signal—from, for argument's sake, that hinterland transect, thousands of light years beyond the Galactic core—was of borderline intensity for detectability at Earth's distance, in which case it could be swamped by a stronger, intervening signal. Which the List of Wealthy Donors supplied itself, indirectly and quite unwittingly.

The mission, in short, had cuckooed itself. It was a giddying thing to contemplate, and not in a good way.

The signal is sent, from far away and far in our Pleistocene past. It arrives on the Earth of five decades past and is marked as the indisputable product of a technically-advanced extraterrestrial civilisation which (perhaps mistakenly, on some now-inaccessible first iteration of the sequence) is determined to lie twenty-six-thousand-odd light-years away, in the neighbourhood of the Galactic core. There is no quick solution, no accessible elucidation of its meaning. Deciphering of the signal proves to be beyond the capabilities of all Earth's experts in such matters. Probes are sent, but fail to return useful information, or indeed themselves. The decision is taken to construct an enormous starship capable of traversing the distance to the centre of the Galaxy, and of carrying a crew with sufficient breadth and depth of knowledge and experience to have, one would hope, a fair chance of successfully initiating two-way conversation with any technologically advanced race they meet. But, partway through the five-year voyage, the pottos escape—

She needed to backtrack. There was a connection here. The pottos were highly intelligent, but they were highly intelligent only because Sal Hinkley had in some manner bioengineered superintelligence into them. (Which meant, if this was all some kind of fey twenty-six-thousand-year loop, then Sal was as integral a part of it as were the pottos…)

So. The pottos escape, try first to carve out a hidden niche for themselves within the List's ventilation shafts and crawlspaces. They develop the beginnings of their own language. But one of them overhears an audio transmission of the signal, realises it sounds familiar… it is, in fact, the pottos' own language, which can only be possible if the pottos themselves had sent the signal, those many centuries ago, which plainly is not possible. But, having recently killed the author Kit Warburton in a thwarted bid for dietary protein, the pottos find themselves in possession of her most recent manuscript, which carries the somewhat unwieldy title of How To Construct Your Own Fully Functional Time Machine From Widely-Available Spacecraft Parts. *Which the pottos then do, because why would you not? And, armed with a bewilderingly modified time-travel-capable shuttle, the List's plundered seed bank and gene library and every useful gadget they can lay their thieving little hands on, they desert the* List of Wealthy Donors. *They have with them the List's primary radio transmitter and enough of Warburton's multitudinous pop-tech how-to guides to enable them to convert said radiotransmitter into an instrument capable of sending a powerful signal across twenty-six thousand light-years of untidy high vacuum. They take this radio transmitter and the heavily-modified shuttle* Exceptional Sponsorship Opportunities *with them twenty-six thousand years into the past and…*

The signal is sent. And it all happens again. Only it doesn't feel like 'again', because time loops are weird, and undetectable to those who inhabit them.

Karinette felt giddy simply thinking about it. But she couldn't not think about it, about the way in which the pottos had cheated them all.

For the time loop to happen, it requires the pottos. It requires the participation of Sal Hinkley, because otherwise the pottos don't get to be superintelligent. It requires the collective participation of a very large number of humans, to propose and design and construct the List of Wealthy Donors, *which provides the vehicle through which the time loop propagates itself. None of those are essential, perhaps, because those nuts and bolts would have been assembled by someone else if one of those individuals hadn't participated... it's all dependent, ultimately, on Sal Hinkley and the pottos. And on Kit Warburton, whose truly bodacious breadth of knowledge, outstanding science-communication skills and freakish productivity ensure that the small band of pottos have all the conceptual equipment they need to make their escape through time. Each time the time loop runs.*

Sal Hinkley. Kit Warburton. And a half-dozen fiendishly smart pottos, all of them dead or as good as dead at this end of their twenty-six-thousand-year spree. The only potto remaining on board, Pansy, is for some reason a discard. No wonder she—

Karinette froze in mid-contemplation. She had just remembered something, a conversation four or more years ago with her now-deceased friend. Sal had been complaining of a lack of motivation, of a concern at not being able to know whether any research he would achieve on board would genuinely be innovative, and not pre-emptively duplicated in his absence, by the time the *List* finally returned to Earth a decade hence. He'd been, in short, in a proper funk. And she'd advised him, more-or-less on the moment's spur, to—

To reach for the overly ambitious, the probably unattainable.

Well, he'd certainly done that.

She was as much responsible for the pottos, and the time loop, as was Sal. The effort in bioengineering the little primates was all his, but the spark had been hers. If she had but advised him differently—

She'd found common ground, of a sort, with Pansy. Dr Karinette Lichtermann was a key, if very minor, part of the time loop. It wasn't a comforting thought.

She was, indeed, a cogwheel.

*

Stef Chandrasekhar, Captain (Third Shift) of the *List of Wealthy Donors* and Captain (Sole Command) of the *Bob's Budget Hovercar Repairs* had decided, within an hour of the commencement of Lichtermann's descent, that there was little advantage to remaining on the platform. Consequently, she'd returned, accompanied by the historian, to the shuttle drifting alongside the alien artefact. From there she could report more straightforwardly to those on the *List*. It also afforded her the opportunity to worry about the prospects for catastrophic failure of makeshift repairs to physical objects rather than concern herself with the permanence, or otherwise, of inexplicable alien forcefield technology. She had to admit, being back on the shuttle felt intrinsically more comfortable; there was always something distinctly unsettling about magical physics, particularly when it effectively held one's life in its inscrutable, insubstantial grasp. It had seemed prudent, nonetheless, to maintain a presence of some description on the platform, to monitor for any developments which might not be apparent from the shuttle itself, and Gandel Urkhart fulfilled that obligation very satisfactorily, He could communicate with Lichtermann should the need and the capability arise—the two presumably would have a reasonable rapport after five years' collaborative training together, although there'd been few opportunities to gauge body language on the cramped flight from the *List* to planetary orbit—and she had to admit that she, personally, found his proximity a little distasteful. This was, perhaps, more on her than on him, but in any event, it was well that he had so obligingly accepted the suggestion that someone should remain on the alien platform. He really was a strange bird. Though the same, she supposed, could equally be said of Lichtermann as well. Perhaps it was just that the field of xenolinguistics tended to attract that sort.

Chandrasekhar had naturally expected that the hours and days immediately following Yolande's deactivation would be the most winnowing, the most exacting she would ever have to face. It had most definitely been an arduous and occasionally terrifying time. But those duty cycles, when the mere survival of each and every human aboard the *List* had been thrown into question, had at least seen the crew labour in unison towards a common end. What she faced now was not (or at least, not obviously) peril, but something more innately problematic: risk. She had had thrust on her shoulders, those three weeks past, a decision for which neither she, nor any other person on board the *List*, had any relevant experience, and therefore she had no way of knowing whether the choice she had made—which was to keep the fateful information close to her chest, and to confide only in those whom she could trust to do likewise—had been the correct course. In all probability, there was no correct course, for how does one treat the news that a singularly costly and intensive diplomacy-and-science mission has been reduced to a mockery through actions initiated during the voyage? She just knew that a statement released could not effectively be retracted, and so she'd kept schtum. She could not stand before the entire crew of the *List*, could not see them all gazing expectantly, rapt, awaiting news about the intended contact mission, and say to them: "Actually, pottos." She just couldn't. And yet she might well have to, at the end of all this. Unless Lichtermann did it for her. And even then there would surely be questions about what she, Chandrasekhar, had known, and what the other Captains had known. It would inevitably tarnish the position of Captain, in the eyes of the personnel. Worse—or no, not worse, because that would be an unconscionably self-centred attitude; but nonetheless still bad, regardless of how it was sliced—was the manner in which this development, the potto development, would play into the burgeoning power struggle between shifts. The arrangement of a tripartite command structure, each facet holding sway and responsibility across eight hours of every daycycle, had worked smoothly (matters of chair height excepted) while there was, effectively, one entity in continuous command and control. With Yolande's termination, that governing mechanism no longer operated, and the routine of it was losing its operational momentum. Squabbles had begun to break out, disagreements, between the engineers, between the navigators, between the captains. Principally, of course, between Rodriquez and Styring; she'd always endeavoured to stay aloof from such pettiness, and for the most part she'd succeeded, had even won for herself a small reputation as a peacemaker of sorts. She now dreaded the manner in which this potto imbroglio would present Styring and Rodriquez with something substantial to unite them, against her. She should've seen this, should've acted accordingly. But it was too late now to recognise this, too late to appropriately rectify it.

It was going to be a long journey back.

There was, she supposed, one slender saving grace. The orbiting platform, the umbilicus, the elevator were active structures: there had been automated responses to their arrival, which suggested that the pottos' tenancy here had been ongoing, and at least recent if not still enduring. Chandrasekhar had had some doubts (actually they had been Pernillesdottir's doubts, but Stef had absorbed them as her own, as would any commander worth her

148

salt when confronted by informed advice from a subordinate) as to whether Hinkley's engineered superintelligence had been a heritable commodity among the pottos. It was entirely feasible that their sapience would have died with the generation of Pansy's crechemates, not passed on to their descendants. The umbilicus and the elevator strongly suggested that there hadn't been a reversion to what she supposed she would have to consider as the animal state. Which was something to be thankful for, provided one was willing to extend the attribute of thankibility to something possessing many of the less desirable characteristics of a double-edged sword.

They'd get a definitive answer on that, soon. Probably.

"So do we just jolly well wait?" Gandel asked, over the radio.

"Not a lot else we can do," Laramie replied, swivelling in her seat to roll her eyes at the Captain and Hamdi. "Unless there's any movement at the station."

"Movement at what dashed station?" Gandel asked.

"Professor, if the isolation is getting to you, you're more than welcome to come across to the shuttle," Chandrasekhar felt obliged to say, ignoring the vigorous head-shakes that the pilot and the historian offered at this juncture. "But as Laramie has indicated, there doesn't seem to be anything we can do beyond wait for further developments."

"I can't understand why Lichtermann hasn't reported back," he complained. "She's generally highly conscientious." He paused. "Irascible, but conscientious."

"She probably can't," said Laramie. "The signal strength from her transmitter wouldn't be strong enough for us to detect it."

"Well, why jolly well not?"

Chandrasekhar leaned in to the microphone again. "Because this contact mission isn't proceeding the way we had imagined it would. I'd have thought, Professor, that you of all people would be in a position to understand that inherent unpredictability."

"I don't think you're taking this seriously enough. Karinette is down there on that dashed planet, utterly alone with heavens only knows what kind of bally alien creatures, and you're jolly well making out that all we need to do is wait?"

"Your concern for your colleague's wellbeing does you credit, Professor," said Chandrasekhar, who then melded a little more steel into her voice. "But Lichtermann is a professional, and I have to believe that she is doing everything she can to foster the success of this contact mission."

She turned a warning eye to Hamdi, who had shown signs of preparing to interject. "Besides, it's not a matter of waiting is all we *need* to do. We are currently dependent on the aliens' goodwill, at least insofar as Lichtermann is concerned: waiting is all we *can* do. We have no means of reaching the surface ourselves, unless they send us such a means. And they haven't."

Chandrasekhar was growing steadily more sure that they wouldn't. And she didn't know what that would signify.

Daycycle 1962

This is a disaster. A mockery. We've allowed the most ambitious scientific mission in all of human history to get hijacked by a mishap, a side project of our own creation.

She needed not to think like this. She needed detachment, equanimity, dignity. Resilience. Wherever Karinette might hope to find any of that within herself, particularly now that she had recollected her own inadvertent part in engineering this situation.

It was morning; the descent had consumed the night. The elevator car was dropping much more slowly now, its wraparound wall and ceiling transparent once more. Sky blue, scraps of cloud. Strong sunlight. Alien planet. She tried to convince herself on that last point; it was surprisingly difficult. *You know who to expect*, she told herself. *You just don't know what to expect.*

It had not been meant to be this way, but it was this way. She smiled, surprising herself, at the incongruous memory of a rubber-costumed McGillivray. *What a waste of creative visualisation that all was*, she thought. *This looks nothing like the lang lab role-plays. I'd always said it wouldn't.*

It would happen. The immediate future was unknown. That part, at least, rang true. That part was as it should be. Perhaps it was all as it should be. Just because it felt like a cheat, to her, did not mean that it was a cheat. It was a wrinkle, a complication. Ancient history. Those in the forested landscape below would have moved on. Perhaps it was time for her to do likewise, even if to do so felt disloyal. It wasn't reasonable, frankly, to expect herself to let go of the deaths of Sal and Yolande and the others, which had occurred mere months or weeks ago. Conversely, it was blatantly unfair to hold any sense of blame or culpability against the unfathomably distant descendants of her crewmates' killers, however natural or correct it felt to her, a human adult, to do so. She was confronted, therefore, with the most difficult, most weighty decision she might ever have to make. To conciliate seemed akin to adopting victimhood, and to excusing the actions of criminals; to seek retribution or to claim grievance would be, from the perspective of twenty-six thousand years' remove, the height of pettiness. There were no rule-books for this situation; merely her decision, which would carry consequences far beyond her own gut feelings, her own prejudices, her own sense of snarky vulnerability. "You Are Here," she told herself, in the obligatory roboticised tones associated with the catchphrase; and smirked. And was surprised to find, after all, that only one choice of action was possible.

So she chose it.

It felt rushed to do so, but that couldn't be helped. From where she was travelling, it was always going to feel rushed.

She hadn't trained for this. But she'd trained for something very like this, and perhaps it was as simple, frankly, as telling herself that this was what she'd trained for. And she'd trained for *that*.

Karinette could see trees beneath her, looming nearer. Individual trees with boughs and lush green foliage. Individual boughs with leaf-fisted branches radiating off them. Individual branches with small furry shapes moving nimbly along them. Individual small furry shapes, pottos, intrigued, attentive, a wide-eyed audience clinging to branches beneath her; alongside her; above her. The forest's overarching canopy stippling the sunlight. Highlights glinting off the metallic casings of a few small lenticular devices adhering to, or embedded within, the trees' trunks. Baby pottos clinging to their parents' backs. The sight calmed her, briefly. *But even dangerous animals procreate. We can't all be bonobos.*

The elevator capsule stopped its descent. Pansy, she could feel, was trembling within the hard-cased pet carrier, though to what end she didn't know. It might well be anticipation, or anxiety, or terror, or excretory desperation, or some arbitrary combination of these. Should she let her out?

Karinette's heart was thumping, her tongue heavy and useless in her mouth. Words that had suggested themselves to her, on her descent, now seemed trite, out of place. Not suited to this place. Besides which, she still didn't know the language, although she had an interpreter in the pet carrier. Provided the interpreter's nerves didn't fail. Provided those they were about to meet still remembered the primordial tongue of their potto ancestors.

It was the elevator capsule which spoke first. "Are you ready for some introductions, Dr Lichtermann?"

Karinette's eyes welled up. She knew that voice; had never expected to hear it again. If the pottos had kept a pirated copy of her friend safe and sane across more than two dozen millennia, then perhaps there was hope for rapprochement between the tribes of small and large primates. Was it possible that this society, this as-yet-unfathomed world, was not just an ill-born product of Sal Hinkley's restless scientific curiosity, but an enduring and fitting tribute to it? A legacy? Twenty-six thousand years was, after all, a lot of time for maturation; for self-reflection; for growth. They didn't seem to have trashed their planet in that span, based on what had been visible from atop the atmosphere and judging by the forested environs around the now-grounded elevator car. Were these creatures—these people—truly as peaceable, now, as this setting suggested? She supposed she'd find out. Maybe they'd learnt things that humanity still hadn't, about themselves and about how to be... which, she supposed, was what had always been hoped for, amongst those who had ridden all this way on the *List of Wealthy Donors*; those for whom she now found herself in the awkward position, for now, of being the sole representative present. Time to do them proud, if it was within her capacity to do so. Get this over with, and she could worry after that about what she would be able to pass on to the others in orbit and to the crowd waiting back aboard the *List*. Regardless of how this went, there would be some explaining to do; but perhaps there'd be a way to sell it, a way for it to seem less than a total derailment of first-contact expectation. Maybe she would even be able to convey it as a success. She coughed, cleared her throat. Lifted her chin a little. "Call me Karinette, please. Yolande. Yes, I guess I'm ready. Goodness, it's been a while, hasn't it? How have things been?"

It wasn't the first-contact statement dictated by the mission guidelines, was nowhere near a form of words worthy of recording in the history books as humanity's first official pronouncement to a long-established extraterrestrial society; but posterity, frankly, could go get bent.

She dabbed a little moisture away from her eye. She'd wing this, and hope it went okay.

Once that door opened, she would become the first human ever to encounter an advanced alien technological civilisation of twenty-six thousand years' standing. She had no way to know how it would go.

She would just need to play it as it came.

Epilogue

(or Afterword, if you prefer)

Three years later, fourteen thousand light years further on

Grrrphth growled. Its race was long-lived, and possessed of an almost geological sense of patience, but this had gone on just too bloody long. Where *were* they?

The trap, so carefully prepared, so painstakingly maintained, lay empty. Still.

For now.

Acknowledgements

This book is indebted in a sense—though not a monetary sense—to the NaNoWriMo process; for it was begun during NaNoWriMo, which for those who have not heard of it is a kind of scheme or game or self-torture process whereby one tries, within the space of one month—November—to write a fifty-thousand-word novel which, plus change, is about what this book is. Was it completed during NaNoWriMo? Well, no. But if one takes a highly elastic definition of the concept of 'November' to which a hefty dollop of time dilation—about eleven years' worth—has been applied, and if one doesn't look too closely, it might just about seem to squeeze in. So thanks, NaNoWriMo. You at least got the thing started, and that's not nothing.

There are actual people to thank, also. I am particularly grateful to James Morrison for the care and thoroughness of his editing, and for his wonderful cover image.

Heartfelt thanks also to Margaret Morgan and Craig Cormick for their support; to Chris Large for showing early interest in the story (and for occasionally asking whether the thing was finished yet); to Gillian Polack for noting inexactitudes in the story's representation of linguistic endeavour; and to Tycho, Brin, and Sue for not begrudging me the time taken to assemble the thing.

Of course, nobody reads acknowledgements nowadays, so I can safely assert here that any defects still remaining in the book are naturally the responsibility of an as-yet-unidentified scapegoat.

About the Author

Born and raised in North Canterbury, New Zealand, Simon Petrie now lives in Canberra, Australia, where he is paid to be careful with words. He has been shortlisted several times for the Sir Julius Vogel, Ditmar, and Aurealis Awards, and has won the Sir Julius Vogel Award three times: in 2010 for Best New Talent and in 2013 and 2018, with *Flight 404* and *Matters Arising from the Identification of the Body* respectively, for Best Novella. He also scored a coveted Dishonourable Mention in the 2011 Bulwer-Lytton Fiction Contest.

He has edited five issues (numbers 35, 40, 51, 54, and 61) of *Andromeda Spaceways Inflight Magazine*, and has co-edited two anthologies (*Light Touch Paper, Stand Clear* and *Use Only As Directed*) with Edwina Harvey and one (*Next*) with Rob Porteous. Though he has produced five short-story collections to date (and is actively preparing a sixth), this is somehow his first novel.

Also by Simon Petrie

Light levels are low. It's killingly cold. These conditions are, it transpires, connected.

The icy landscape around you—hillocks, boulders, ravines, foregrounding a hazy, rumpled horizon beneath an opaque, lowering sky—wears a patina that shades from sepia to umber, puddled with drifts of dark sand. The atmosphere, though thick, would permit only a parody of respiration: there is no succour in it. Were it not for the insulating, carefully-regulated containment of your suit, you would be dead within minutes, frozen solid within an hour.

Welcome to Titan.

Wide Brown Land: stories of Titan is a collection of eleven hard-SF short stories set on Saturn's most intriguing moon.

•

She took her helmet off.
   That's where it starts; that's where it ends.
   That's all there is.

Tanja Morgenstein, daughter of a wealthy industrialist and a geochemist, is dead from exposure to Titan's lethal, chilled atmosphere, and Guerline Scarfe must determine why.

This novella blends hard-SF extrapolation with elements of contemporary crime fiction, to envisage a future human society in a hostile environment, in which a young woman's worst enemies may be those around her.

Matters Arising from the Identification of the Body is a Sir Julius Vogel Award winning SF / mystery novella.

Amorous space squids. Sentient fridges. A derelict alien spacecraft adrift within an interstellar cloud. Speed-dating zombies. The truth behind the extinction of the dinosaurs. A potentially lethal interasteroidal freight consignment. And a planet on which biological diversification has utterly failed to take hold in eight billion years.

80,000 Totally Secure Passwords That No Hacker Would Ever Guess is a misleadingly-named collection of SF short fiction, sometimes humorous and sometimes deadly serious. While several of these stories have previously appeared in the earlier collections *Rare Unsigned Copy* and *Difficult Second Album*, this new collection also includes a significant amount of newer fiction.

●

Gordon Mamon was the lift operator in a hotel that didn't have a lift.
The hotel, the 'Skyward Suites 270', was the lift.

All Gordon wants to do, when he isn't delivering room service, administering first aid, washing dishes, cleaning bathrooms, or forwarding service complaints, is to be able to finish his crossword in piece. But people keep inconsiderately dying of unnatural causes during their stay aboard his lift-module on the Skyward space elevator.

Welcome to Module 270, an orbit-transiting hotel with a suspiciously high body count.

Murder on the Zenith Express: the Gordon Mamon collection comprises six not-completely-serious SF mysteries.

●

'They're dead. They're all dead.'
The comment, innocent of deeper intent, is on the flowers withering in a glass vase. But there's a flash of panic, in response, that I only perceive on later re-examination.

The search for a missing interstellar passenger vessel brings investigator Charmain Mertz back to the unwelcoming world of her boyhood.

Flight 404 is a Sir Julius Vogel Award winning SF / mystery novella.